THE LE

SERIES TITLES

What We Might Become
Sara Reish Desmond

The Waterman
Gary Schanbacher

Signs of the Imminent Apocalypse and Other Stories
Heidi Bell

The Silver State Stories
Michael Darcher

Close Call
Kim Suhr

An Instinct for Movement
Michael Mattes

The Machine We Trust
Tim Conrad

Gridlock
Brett Biebel

Salt Folk
Ryan Habermeyer

The Commission of Inquiry
Patrick Nevins

Maximum Speed
Kevin Clouther

Reach Her in This Light
Jane Curtis

The Spirit in My Shoes
John Michael Cummings

The Effects of Urban Renewal on Mid-Century America and Other Crime Stories
Jeff Esterholm

What Makes You Think You're Supposed to Feel Better
Jody Hobbs Hesler

Fugitive Daydreams
Leah McCormack

Hoist House: A Novella & Stories
Jenny Robertson

Finding the Bones: Stories & A Novella
Nikki Kallio

Self-Defense
Corey Mertes

Where Are Your People From?
James B. De Monte

Sometimes Creek
Steve Fox

The Plagues
Joe Baumann

The Clayfields
Elise Gregory

Kind of Blue
Christopher Chambers

Evangelina Everyday
Dawn Burns

Township
Jamie Lyn Smith

Responsible Adults
Patricia Ann McNair

Great Escapes from Detroit
Joseph O'Malley

Nothing to Lose
Kim Suhr

The Appointed Hour
Susanne Davis

PRAISE FOR
WHAT WE MIGHT BECOME

"Sara Reish Desmond's beautiful debut collection provided me with everything I hope to find in a book of stories. Time after time, she grabbed my attention in the opening lines and held it even after I read the final sentence. These stories are vivid and taut, and one of Desmond's great virtues is that she doesn't get in the way of her characters. She lets them breathe. I'll be eager to read her work from now on."

—STEVE YARBROUGH
author of *Stay Gone Days*

"Sara Reish Desmond's *What We Might Become* maps the spaces left in the wake of grief, and all the ways we hunger and search, in that aftermath, to connect, heal, and belong. I cherished these surprising love stories—each of them rendering the tender fallibility of the human heart and our unyielding determination to mend what has been broken. I will return to these haunting, perfect stories, and their evocative landscapes, again and again."

—ROBIN MacARTHUR
author of *Half Wild*

"I love everything about Sara Reish Desmond's *What We Might Become*: the cadence of the sentences, the probing, unsettling voice of her narrators, and the dark conclusions she reaches about the underside of contemporary American life. She writes with quiet fury. Anyone who loves short stories will want to own this one."

—JESS ROW
author of *The New Earth*

"At the heart of Sara Reish Desmond's stories are characters living lives of quiet desperation. They are desperate to be seen, desperate to connect, desperate to be loved and to offer love to others. Desmond does not shy away from this desperation. She confronts it, forces us as her readers to sit with it as well. To consider our own quiet desperation, who it causes us to harm, who it impels us to love. You will not shake these stories easily. I certainly have not."

—NEEMA AVASHIA
author of *Another Appalachia*

WHAT WE MIGHT BECOME

stories

SARA REISH DESMOND

CORNERSTONE PRESS
UNIVERSITY OF WISCONSIN-STEVENS POINT

Cornerstone Press, Stevens Point, Wisconsin 54481
Copyright © 2024 Sara Reish Desmond
www.uwsp.edu/cornerstone

Printed in the United States of America by
Point Print and Design Studio, Stevens Point, Wisconsin

Library of Congress Control Number: 2024942395
ISBN: 978-1-960329-44-8

All rights reserved.

This is a work of fiction. Names, characters, businesses, places, events, and incidents are either the products of the author's imagination or used in a fictitious manner. Any resemblance to actual persons, living or dead, or actual events is purely coincidental.

Cornerstone Press titles are produced in courses and internships offered by the Department of English at the University of Wisconsin–Stevens Point.

DIRECTOR & PUBLISHER
Dr. Ross K. Tangedal

EXECUTIVE EDITORS
Jeff Snowbarger, Freesia McKee

EDITORIAL DIRECTOR
Ellie Atkinson

SENIOR EDITORS
Brett Hill, Grace Dahl

PRESS STAFF
Paige Biever, Sam Bjork, Chloe Cieszynski, Gwen Goetter, Allison Lange, Sophie McPherson, Kylie Newton, Eva Nielsen, Angelina Sherman, Ava Willett

For Matt, Josephine, and Cora

stories

Clay Girls 1

Some Small Act of Compassion 17

C3PGirl 43

The Unseen 55

The Fells 77

Up Dell Drive 91

Cicadas 109

The Dwindling 117

Small Secrets 133

Sickness and Health 143

Pie 157

Acknowledgments 165

Clay Girls

If she could do it over, Elise wouldn't tell her son, Sam, that he'd almost had a sister. She would resist the closeness she felt when Sam smiled adoringly and told her he liked the sculpture of the girl with the Moon Pie eyes because it reminded him of his girlfriend, Lucy (though he could not tell her, serious girl that she was). And because in that moment, her son had smiled sideways like the sly man he was becoming, and because she felt it a privilege to consort with him, Elise had been inclined to tell secrets, too. But she had not adequately considered the risk.

Now, Elise relates that moment to sculpture. She contemplates the difficulty in allowing something to become what it wants and in respecting when to step away. If she could revise the past, she would simply take her sculptures out of the room she'd given over to him, the one that had been her studio, and leave Sam scratching at the newness of his beard, a beard that wasn't quite a beard yet, after all.

This housing arrangement—the swapping of Elise's garage art studio with Sam's room—had been devised in lieu of buying Sam a car. Though she had been reluctant, her husband Dean argued that the move might give her a fresh artist's perspective, a room with more light, like a real gallery space. This morning, when she found Sam's clothes cooling in the dryer, she considered leaving them there so he would come into the house to get them, putting himself in the path of her domestic orbit so that they might talk. She wouldn't care who spoke first. She wasn't sure what she'd say. *I shouldn't have told you...?* That wasn't right. *I was selfish. I'm sorry I upset you...?* Maybe. Instead, she folded his clothes and carried them across the expanse of lawn and up the garage stairs where she now stands inspecting her pale image in the glass of his new bedroom door—eyes tired, short hair flattened by sleep. Even though in her head she hears Dean's subtle admonitions—*reserve is important in the wake of mistakes*—and even as she tries to resist, she cannot keep herself from turning the doorknob. She is comforted to find it locked. She places the laundry basket on the platform outside his door and notices the chalky dots of gray clay still on the railing—a residue of clay girls bathing in the sun.

In the kitchen, she makes a cup of tea and thinks she'll bake cookies, not to draw Sam inside after soccer practice, but because she wants to put her hands in something. Usually, she would withdraw to the studio, throw clay until it became something unexpected, whatever it wanted to be. But her machines are covered with sheets and sit like iron dinosaurs in her new studio upstairs, surrounded by the neat theater of clay girls whom she cannot face today.

So, Elise stands in the middle of the kitchen, sipping from a homemade mug, a sense of inertia about her—all possibility, no action. She wishes now, as she does in times of tension, that she were far away from the person she has become: far away from perfectly mowed lawns, tennis courts, and single-family homes. She wishes she were dressed in smart city clothes—tights, interesting shoes, a silk scarf around her head, dark lipstick, cutting her way through crowded streets on her way to somewhere more important than anything she might approach from here. It would comfort her now, she realizes, to be doing something that makes her feel unlike herself. She wonders for a moment if she might enjoy the routine of an office job (a commute to a design firm, meetings and presentations, interacting with coworkers). She wants it only because she can imagine it to be a successful act of will, unlike the bungled conversation with Sam, an act of impulse. Forty-three years old, no job since Sam was born. The child she lost would be twelve. When the doctors removed the fetus, the size of a grapefruit, they told her the sex, the thing most heartbreaking of all: a girl.

ACROSS TOWN AT KENNEDY MIDDLE SCHOOL, Cheryl Boyd is watching as Mr. Moran tries to simulate the melting of the polar ice caps with a hot plate and ice cubes. He has not created enough surface tension before he begins the demonstration; she can tell that even from her place three deep behind the smaller, well-liked students in her class. After school today, she hopes to walk home with Carmen DeRossi. Carmen's older brother, Ian, knows a tricky way into the computer sites his parents block and some days they watch raunchy videos of college kids getting drunk and taking their clothes off, doing things she's never seen. She and Carmen make popcorn or share a bag of Cheetos and climb into Carmen's bed, under the covers, their eyes unblinking, their foreheads wrinkling, their eyebrows raised in amazement. Sometimes, when Carmen goes to refill their drinks or use the bathroom, Ian, who always smells a little bit like rubber, sits down on the bed next to Cheryl and runs his hands over her legs.

Once, he came over for a handful of M&Ms and put his face so close to hers she could feel the heat of his cheek and then he stuck out his tongue and drew the tip of it along the base of her neck, up her chin and into her ear. She tensed every muscle in her body and squeezed her eyes tight and when he was done, he stood there just smelling her, in that humid place between hair and earlobe, until Carmen swung open the door and Ian made the fine, flawless transition back to the M&Ms. It had happened only that once, and another time when she wasn't sure if the elevator was just small or if he intended to rest his hand on her ass as they rode up to the second floor of the Silverpeak Mall. But still—it had taught her something about what she thought she was and what she could be.

EVEN AFTER TWELVE YEARS, the possibility of that girl-child freezes Elise in time at least once a day so that she is losing time. She watches the Oriole beating its wings in the garden bath, she thinks *fluttering heart*—two minutes gone. The car idling in the driveway, the pitch of radio static telling her names—*Clementine, Leona, Tessa*—another three minutes gone. In lost intervals such as these, the girl looks like Elise, or Dean, or a girl-Sam, or none of them. Today she is freckled and ebony-haired—the thick black braids pulled so tight her face must hurt. Fantasy is memory and forgetting all at once, and Elise cannot tell the difference between them. She has marked every year of the child's death with a new clay girl and has given each girl a name, has pushed the clay into the girl it wants to be. This year is the year of Rosaline. She'd written the name in pencil beneath Tessa and Clementine and Lily in a neat patch on the wall next to her potter's wheel, slicking a fresh coat of white paint over it when the room became Sam's.

Elise had spent the last few days finding places for each of the twelve clay figures. Two were so gloomy that she packaged them in Styrofoam peanuts and placed them in the garage. But Lily, her hands behind her back, her face thrust forward as if holding a secret she was proud to know, had hair down to her feet and wore a wreath of flowers on her head. Elise had been particularly proud of the effect of lightness in the girl's hair, that one large slab of clay she'd painstakingly carved and fussed over until she'd gotten it right. Each of the girls possessed a caricature feature (a minute mouth, huge feet, fruit for hair), each one of them a bittersweet memorial.

THE DAY SHE MOVED THE STUDIO, Sam had come through the door in the moment she was considering the length of Lily's hair, her small waist, how sculpture can be both building and taking away.

"Mom?" he'd said, startling her.

"Oh, hi Sam. I'm gathering the last of it."

"Don't worry. Take your time." He had shown a unique affection in the weeks since she and Dean had promised him the room, a response to his mother's sacrifice, and she was taken by his sweetness.

"Where should I put that one?" she had asked, pointing to Clementine, who held a bowl of her namesake fruit on her head.

"I don't know. The kitchen?"

She nodded. "We'll see what your father thinks."

When he was eight, Sam had made a clay boy for his mother, likely a self-portrait with long, spindly arms and an oversized head. Elise used it in the sculpture of Leona—she had placed it in the clay girl's cupped hands so that Leona became a clay girl holding a small clay boy named Sam.

Moving the last of his boxes into the studio, Sam had said, "I've always liked this one." He had pointed to the knee-high, pot-bellied Leona, her shirt riding above her belly button, her eyes wide as Moon Pies as she offers the boy to the sky to join his real, lost sister there.

"Leona." She had felt camaraderie in their discussion—the way discovery brings together uncommon people.

"She looks like a Leona."

"Yeah. I think so, too. Do you remember when you made that boy for me?"

"Not really."

"You brought him home and told me you made it for the little girls I sculpted."

He had tried to look sensitive in that moment, she thought, which had made her feel pitiful.

"You want to keep this one up here, in your room?" The smallest part of her had considered the chance that he might like to have something she made—it didn't matter the reason—novelty, curiosity, something else she could not imagine. The largest part of her had wanted to explain herself to him. "Never mind, I'm sorry. I'll find…"

"No, Mom. I mean…" Sam had given Leona a kid-sisterly pat on the head. She imagined his friends responding to the sculpture: *Cool fat girl, man. Is Lucy jealous?*

"I'm sorry. Never mind."

"Mom, it's no big deal. It's just that she kind of reminds me of Lucy. I know they don't look alike but…"

While he paused, the blood had rushed up in Elise's eardrums, like butterfly wings beating against her brain. He was right. Even though Sam's girlfriend is rail thin and looks nothing like Leona, something about her intensity had been captured in the clay. Sam's acumen had unsteadied her, and the beating wings had grown louder so that she could not resist the demand of it, could not deny the temptation to make sense of her sadness, her distance, her disappointment, if that's what it was.

"Sam, when you were small, I lost a baby. A little girl." Sam had suddenly withdrawn his hand. "I want you to know that now. You're old enough." Something fired and faded behind his eyes, the way a light bulb blows and dies as the circuit connects with a flipped switch.

"I would've had a sister?"

"Do you remember that I was pregnant when you were small?"

His face was expressionless. "Should I?" He sat down hard on his bed. The room smelled of damp clay. Leona's cartoon eyes, watching them like that, grew sad. "Why are you telling me this?"

"I'm trying my best here, Sam."

"To do what?"

"To be honest." Elise moved between Sam and Leona, like an eclipse.

"Why?"

"Shouldn't I be?"

"You think that's gonna help me? Or is it going to make *you* feel better?"

In the four days since this discussion, Sam had floated between the garage and the house like some ancient spirit, knowing too much. When he came inside for meals, he engaged in small talk with Dean but never so much as glanced in Elise's direction. She couldn't even know if it was confusion or resentment or sadness that made him seem, suddenly, like a clay boy too, the product of someone else's hands. This morning, she had seen him bound down the garage stairs, his untucked shirt and backpack trailing behind him on the way to school.

Elise hadn't told Dean until last night. She knew he'd disapprove, blame her impetuosity, which had been a point of attraction when they'd first met but now irritated them both—Elise chastising herself afterward and Dean thinking her irrational and self-absorbed.

"What were the circumstances?" Dean asked.

"It just happened. We were talking like we hadn't in a long time and I thought it would help him understand."

"Understand what?"

"Understand me." She hated hearing herself say it. Now Dean could call her narcissistic, too.

"And how did it go?"

She wanted to tell him but couldn't.

That night, Dean had waited on the couch for Sam to join him until the end of the third inning of the baseball game. When he didn't arrive, Dean took the iPad out to the garage to join Sam. There, Dean had fallen asleep so Elise had awoken alone this morning, exiled by both husband and son.

Now, she retrieves a worn index card from her recipe box and measures flour and sugar into a large bowl. School would be letting out soon.

WHEN CHERYL BOYD JOSTLES HER WAY through the steady stream of back-packed middle-schoolers and pushes open the heavy doors into the bright afternoon, she links arms with Carmen DeRossi who is also a Girl Scout in troop 439. As a team, they unexpectedly spot the Boyd family minivan and Cheryl's mother standing before it, her arms crossed. Cheryl senses the need for reinforcement. Her mother does not look at Cheryl and instead directs her business to Carmen. "Today is not the day, Carmen. Go home."

Cheryl learns that this morning, when her mother had been reorganizing Cheryl's closet, hanging up her freshly ironed Girl Scout uniform, she had discovered something: the green flap of a Thin Mint box sticking out between two of Cheryl's locked diaries. She had removed them to find exactly twenty-three neatly collapsed boxes and a stack of greasy plastic trays. Her mother has brought this evidence and placed it on the passenger seat. Cheryl imagines that her mother expects the very sight of these cookie boxes and plastic trays will have her sobbing in a matter of minutes. As her mother guides the minivan out of the parking lot in silence, Cheryl braces for her to blow like a volcano, which her mother does when she feels she's been humiliated. Her mother is measured about *how* she chooses to blow and *where*. She is a private woman who likes to maintain an image of control, though Cheryl would argue she likes to maintain an image of perfection. The silence is the prolonged percolation of lava in her mother's veins.

Her mother is likely considering who Cheryl has duped. Cheryl could tell her: there are the Stevensons and the Bennets and the Franginis, all of whom dutifully order more than a half dozen boxes each year. In her consumption, she had at least enough sense to eat the cookies of the people on the fringe, the people who will not remember writing the check, who winced when they answered the door to find this pudgy, sullen twelve-year-old peddling cookies in her green vest. She hadn't considered any of that. She'd simply eaten them all.

"Tell me about the boxes at your feet, Cheryl."

"They're Girl Scout cookie boxes, Mother."

"And where, pray tell, might the missing cookies be?"

"I ate the Donahue's order first, while I watched *America's Most Wanted* on the TV you and Dad think is broken but still gets local channels."

HER MOTHER'S JAW DROPS. Cheryl is not permitted to watch graphic content. If her mother had her way, Cheryl would watch nothing that doesn't directly promote the values of the Scouts: Discover, Connect, Take Action! She could argue that she "discovered" the Thank U Berry Munches that were introduced in the 2023 scouting season and then "connected" and "took action" for the Donahue's by eating their share. Cheryl smiles with delight. Her mother takes a corner fast; the cookie boxes fan out on the floor at Cheryl's feet.

"Cheryl!"

"They were delicious, actually. I approve of the new flavor. You can tell the head honchos in New York that troop 439 awards the new ones two thumbs up. Then, I ate Mrs. Gumpper's Tag-Alongs while watching *American Idol*."

"Oh, you are really something, aren't you? Don't think there aren't consequences for this, Cheryl Elizabeth Boyd." To demonstrate the severity of those consequences, her mother pulls the van over to the edge of an alfalfa field still miles from home. Cheryl supposes maybe she'll be left there to walk—which her mother had done when Cheryl lied to the principal so she could be excused from the duration of the gymnastics unit.

"Count them," her mother says, when the car is still.

"Oh I don't have to. There are twenty-three. Five boxes of Thanks A Lots, four boxes of Daisy Go Rounds, which suck by the way…"

Her mother squeezes Cheryl's plump face with one pink, acrylic-nailed hand. It's clear that she has not rehearsed this. Mrs. Boyd had expected tears not backtalk. But instead, Cheryl feels only pride that she has eaten 41,000 calories of other peoples' cookies.

"Is that so?" her mother says.

Cheryl's face hurts and when her mother finally releases it, her flesh is marked with five tiny crescent moons.

"You want me to walk?" Cheryl asks. Empowered by her new defiance, she relishes it down to the last dramatic drop. Her mother says nothing now. Cheryl has won for the moment, and her mother steers the minivan back onto the road in the direction of home.

Later, her mother pushes Cheryl out the door in full Girl Scout uniform with a photocopied order form in her hand. No, she is not allowed to ride her bike. No, she cannot call them and apologize instead. She must visit every household, every name on the list, until she has explained herself and expressed her regret and made arrangements about the money. She may come home when she's through.

As Cheryl makes her way down the street, she peels off layers of her uniform, one by one. First to go is the hat, perched upon her head like a green paper boat secured with bobby pins. She tosses it into the Donahue's azalea bushes before she rings their doorbell. They are nice enough about the news. She tells them her mother has sent her, there's been some kind of mix-up about the order, they won't be receiving any cookies this year, but thank you for your donation to an organization that cultivates more girl leaders than any other. She smiles and winks, showing her three-fingered salute.

The knee socks are killing her. Her mother makes her wear them for ceremonies and other formal scouting events but they're perhaps even dorkier than the hat. They're too long and must be folded beneath her kneecap, causing dimples in the fat of her knees. When she returns home, her mother will scold her for losing the hat and will frown at her improperly slouched socks, which is why Cheryl drags her vest through the puddle on the Devereaux's walkway. When no one answers, she scrounges in her bag for a scrap of something on which to scratch. On the back of a napkin she writes: *Bon Soir Mdme. Devereaux, The cookies were delicious. Thank you for your support of the Scouts. You Frenchies are all right!*

Next address on her list: The Olsons. She knows a Sam Olson who goes to the high school and has a wide-eyed, pouty girlfriend, but she doesn't remember who placed the order. As she clicks down the brick walkway, Cheryl prepares another lie. *Bankruptcy*. She could design a bogus letterhead and write to inform every loyal cookie fan that the Girl Scout Association of America has fallen on hard times. It's clever. And it requires little or no follow-up. She rings the doorbell. The woman who answers is wearing an oven mitt.

"Hello?" Elise says to the pudgy, flush-faced girl on her doorstep.

"Mrs. Olson?"

"Yes. I'm Elise Olson."

"I'm Cheryl. The Girl Scout."

"Oh right. I'll grab my checkbook." Elise glances over her shoulder in the direction of the kitchen. She shows the girl her oven mitt and says, "I'm actually baking some cookies myself. Come in a minute. I need to take them out before they burn," but she's already hurried away from Cheryl, left her there in the sun porch with the recycling and the discarded shoes. As Elise withdraws the hot cookies from the oven, she remembers this girl, this Cheryl, the way she seems to remember girls of a certain age, girls who bear no resemblance to the women they might become decades in the future. Months before at one of her son's soccer games, Elise had watched this same girl sitting at a card table behind a cookie box pyramid, her pretty blond friend pushing out the new buds of her breasts and coaching her chubby mate in how to solicit orders: *Cookies! Get your favorite Girl Scout cookies here!*

Now, Elise yells from the kitchen, "Would you like a cookie?"

"Sure."

"Come into the kitchen, um, what did you say your name is?" Elise remembers watching her from the bleachers, watching her more intently than she watched Sam as the girl fidgeted with the waistband of her skirt, yanked it over the bulge of fat at her waist so that Elise missed Sam's only goal of the season. Elise's voyeurism had been made more obvious and awkward by the way she used only one eye to stare between Mark Harris's mother and father, Dean redirecting her gaze back to the field on several occasions.

"My name is Cheryl."

Elise places a few hot sugar cookies on a plate and slides them toward the girl. "Here. Sit down... Cheryl," she says, as if testing the name. "You want milk or something?"

"No that's ok." Elise watches the girl survey the orange kitchen, her large brown eyes taking in the refrigerator plastered with family photographs and artsy postcards.

"So how much do I owe you?" Elise asks. "Cheryl," she adds.

"Ironic, right? You making cookies?" The girl laughs and takes a bite.

"I suppose so, yes."

The girl wipes the crumbs from her mouth. "So… The cookies…" She unfolds a tight wad of paper, smooths it on the counter, and draws her finger down the order form. "It looks like you're waiting on a box of Samoas and a box of Thin Mints."

"Yes," Elise nods.

"May I ask you a question?" The girl is holding her off.

Cheryl is the first girl of her lost daughter's age to sit here, at this island in her orange kitchen. When Elise had ordered the cookies, it was the blond who had done the talking, the directing, the order form supervision. Meanwhile Cheryl, Elise remembers now, had used those eyes to take stock of Elise, to calculate the kind of woman she was, the kind of woman who might be staring at a girl like her.

"What kind of a girl do you think I am?" Cheryl asks.

A clay girl, Elise thinks.

"I mean, if you had to say what kind of a girl I am, based on what you see, what would you say?"

The back of Elise's neck tingles with irritation, and it takes her longer than she'd like to reply. "I think that you're somebody's daughter."

"But…what do you expect of me?" the girl asks, impatiently now. "Me, here, in this stupid uniform, apologizing for eating the cookies you ordered when I'm not really sorry anyway…"

As the girl explains herself, Elise cannot know whether this encounter, this young girl sitting comfortably in her kitchen wiping at her bold mouth with the back of her hand as she bears some part of herself to a stranger, is coincidence or a calibrated response to Elise's own quiet sorrow.

"You're here to tell me you ate my order of cookies?" Elise asks.

"Yeah." The girl is proud.

"Oh. Why?"

"Felt like it. So, what do you think of me, now?" she asks. No, it isn't pride. It is daring proof of her brittle control. Cheryl turns down her eyes. Her face reflects no light. The flesh on her fingers and forearms dimples like freshly worked clay.

"Look, does your mom know you're here? Should we call her?"

The girl brings her thumb and forefinger to the corners of her mouth and wipes away the last of the crumbs. "Yeah. She knows. She sent me."

"Your mom sent you here?"

"To apologize."

"Oh."

Cheryl lifts her head, glues her eyes to Elise's and will not allow her to look away.

"Tell your mom you're forgiven. They're just cookies, you know?" Elise says, looking then to the sculpture of Clementine in the corner, the bowl of fruit teetering awkwardly on her head. Clementine, her nose shining in the halo cast by the overhead lamp, seems to have crept further away from the wall, a slow approach to greet the new girl.

"What's with the little clay girl?" Cheryl asks.

"I made her a few years ago." In isolation, Clementine is cheerfully awkward, which is what Elise had intended. She thinks maybe that's the trick. Isolate the girls or give them away. Don't allow them to line the walls of the new studio, a clay girl army charging forth.

"You made her?"

"Yeah. That's what I do. I'm a sculptor."

"Like, that's your job? You do that every day?"

"I try. I mean, I should." Elise wants to tell the girl that some days all she can do is put her hands in the cool bucket of earth. She almost wants to tell her about the secret she shared with Sam, the news of the lost sister, and that now all she wants to do is tip each girl over, wait for the *thunk* of cracked clay on the ground and the rush of beating wings escaping.

Cheryl looks at her curiously. Elise is a stranger to this girl, a stranger who says less than she expects herself to, which pleases Elise for now.

"Do you have more?" Cheryl asks. "Can I see them?"

Because Elise does not want to say yes nor no, she decides only to turn her body in the direction of the stairs, moves consciously through space as if it were clay and her body were carving a clearer, less complicated path than had been there before. When she reaches the top of the stairs, Elise looks down to see the awkward girl following her, her knees dimpling and flattening as she climbs, her breath audible. In the studio at the end of the hall, the afternoon light beams through the windows in grand rectangles that lose their edges on the floor.

When she sees the sculptures, Cheryl's mouth parts in wonder. The girls look back at her. Cheryl goes to Lily, extending her hand as if considering the length of her hair, but does not touch. Cheryl's green sash has shifted during her stay. Her plump calves are restricted by the tightness of her slouching socks. Her face is full and gleaming. Elise wonders if she is thinking what her own hair might do if it were that long, what her mother might say if she grew it to the ground. The balls of Cheryl's cheeks grow rounder as she smiles. She asks, "How do you decide?"

"Decide what?"

"What each girl gets. How they look."

"I don't decide. It just happens."

Cheryl moves into the room, into the palette of light on the floor, where no sculpture stands. The room swells to life. The girls begin to twitter. Cheryl crosses her arms, sucks in her cheeks, shows the length of her neck for the first time. For a moment, she is clay.

Cheryl turns to Elise. "What will I become?" she asks.

And then again, she is girl.

Some Small Act of Compassion

In the bird shop in Dafeng, De's mother had spent her daughter's most precious years weaving small cages from water reeds, her ears stuffed with cotton. At first, it had been to muffle the incessant birdsong, but it provided a safe retreat from so many things: her husband's criticism, customer solicitation, even the inquiries of her maturing daughter who possessed a boldness she and her husband found shameful. De's father was gone five days a week to the salt mines he owned in the country, so as a young woman with curiosities neither parent could appease, she had grown accustomed to picturing her mother with sawdust instead of blood in her veins and her father, a smooth-running machine with no tics—save his off-set jaw, which he held at a contemptuous angle to the miner's labor, his wife's cooking, De's exam marks. The more her father was away in the country, the more her mother remained in the rear of the shop—turning the sign to "closed" during normal business hours, disengaging, shutting her daughter out.

So when the match dropped, De wondered if the cotton in her mother's ears had been so deep and densely packed that she never heard the gasp of the first catch and burn, the way the sound of flames resembled water as they ate up the paper curtains. Surely her mother must've felt the heat encroaching, deceptively comforting, warming the spots in her bones that had never known warmth. And if her mother *had* sensed the onset, De wondered about just how the fire had taken her—willingly, a volunteer seeking exodus from misery? Afterwards, the squelched coals were still smoldering when De walked home to an empty house, the surviving birds trailing behind her like smoke.

Now, in De and Liwei's fresh-start apartment in Cambridge, at the corner of Harvard and Prospect, each new bird sang a different tune, each one punished her for what had happened that day in Dafeng: as the fire caught, De had been transfixed by its unpredictable course, its relentless pursuit of the dry boards in the modest shop. She found herself awed, though now she thinks "paralyzed," watching the fire climb. De had imagined herself shouting words, but even now she was unsure what, if anything, had escaped her lips: *Mother. Mother. This time you ought to listen. This time I'm telling you what might save your life.*

ABOUT THE FIRE, LIWEI WAS of two minds. It was possible that the dropped match *had* been accidental. But he was the one who maintained that the fire, and De's role in it was largely an act of indifference, if not entirely intentional. Even now that De and Liwei were starting over in the U.S., their salvaged lives were complicated by the uncertainty of that day, by De's impulsivity, her neglect. Liwei's doubt made him handle De too roughly and speak too fiercely. The shadow of the tragedy defined and unnerved them. It reminded them of what a future might hold, a future that had changed in an instant fraught with intent or indecision or carelessness, a future that was now theirs to bungle or master as they might.

THE MORNING DE AND LIWEI moved into the apartment, James had been watching—the view from his apartment like a box in an old theater. He could tell the man and the woman were arguing and knew the nature of it: the fast hands and words of one, the resignation of the other. He could tell who had won, even with his music on and their U-Haul windows sealed. After the fight calmed, James watched them unload and considered, briefly, lending the man a hand with their boxes. But instead, he watched. The woman's hair was cropped neat and boxy in the unnatural shade of orange produced when true black tries for blond. She hung reed birdcages from her arms and carried them across the parking lot and up three flights of stairs to their new apartment. James could hear the birds. There must have been a dozen small ones: finches, leafbirds, canaries, and thrushes, he would come to learn later.

It had been a month since James had elected to quit his job as a lawyer for a corporate firm in Boston. It was the kind of firm that makes a person log his billable hours every six minutes, which took six of its own minutes every hour. They had made this compromise only after he and Lila had dug themselves out of considerable debt and could endure a few months on Lila's income alone. Since he had quit the firm, James no longer wore a watch. Time began to advance in unsteady ways, caving in on itself so that a whole afternoon might be lost to reading a novel, or winding out so ostentatiously in the evenings with Lila that he could not wait for sleep. He had begun to notice the details of things more readily, less consumed with time as he was. He noticed, as he had not before, that Lila had a habit of wrinkling her brow so that a crease had formed between her eyebrows above the bridge of her nose. It had deepened since he'd left his job, so that now, even when she sat drinking coffee at the counter, with the full intensity of the new day's sun on her face, the wrinkle remained.

When they were first married, James and Lila scoffed at older pairs sitting silently through uninspired routines. At a restaurant, if they would find themselves seated near an older couple, they would both be disturbed by that couple's complicity, the way a long-weathered pair gave easily into silence as they flaked their sensible salmon into their mouths and drank their chardonnay. James and Lila interpreted silence of this kind as inevitable resignation. It made them shift in their seats. So they would go home in spite, in defiance, in (their own version of) love—sex in the stairwell, winter boots still laced tight, and go at it again in the middle of the night as they both woke for a drink of water, this time hoping they did not need to prove anything to anyone.

They had been married seven years now. They had settled on child-free lives. They yielded to very little and did not understand their own irony, the complicity that had given way in each of them, that had taken hold of them like the roots of a tree around a fencepost. They had settled into their own routine: simple nightly dinners, Sunday lap swim at the Y; reading in bed before their heads bobbed, turning out their bedside lamps. Each of them took to arousing themselves in private ways—Lila as she lay beside James, secure that he was sleeping, James in the shower, and now with greater frequency that he was home alone most days. When they did make love, James was tender and Lila pensive, he without the appetite that would draw her out of her intensity, her hard-working, hard-thinking, hard to come spirit.

LIWEI EXITED THE TRAIN at Kendall Square, two stops from home, so that as he walked, the fresh air might dissolve what it could of the greasy restaurant odors that hung on his clothes and followed him everywhere: to his towels and bed sheets, even to De's own clothing when she sat next to him eating a late supper on the couch. One night, when he came home, De was on the fire escape, wrapped in one of her mother's shawls, smoking again.

"Can I have one of those?" he asked, stepping through the open window to join her. The Mandarin words sounded like rubber bands on a homemade drum.

"*You* want one? All you do is criticize me for smoking," she answered in English.

"It's such a strange habit to take up *now*."

"*Jin tian?* Now that what?"

"Now that she is gone. Now that you say all you smell is smoke."

Even in this new apartment, three months after the fire in Dafeng, when Liwei cooked huiguorou, De's favorite, she said she couldn't even smell the bean paste, she could only smell smoke. Not the enticing smoke of cigarettes but the smoke of dry wood and dust, of absence and silence and stagnation. She had made clear the distinction to Liwei, who thought of her smoking as an effort to blot out one incineration with another.

"It's different," she insisted.

"You've said."

She stubbed out the cigarette and leaned over the fire escape to watch the traffic pass on Prospect Street. She was momentarily energized by the commotion of the city, had longed for it even, having left the bustle of her hometown in China. And now that she was here, she was most content to be inside, to watch the city from a distance.

"You were just out there that day with the birds?" Liwei asked again as he had so many times since the fire, hoping another inquiry would give way to new information.

"Yes, Li," she urged, calling him his American name. She *had* failed to call the authorities even though neighbors did. What they found when they arrived on the scene was a dry-eyed girl (the newspapers had called her *girl*, a woman of 23!) watching the flames, surrounded by cages, birds resting on her shoulders and folded arms.

"And you didn't try to go back in? You didn't try…"

"You weren't there. It went up so fast."

"Couldn't you hear her? She must've…"

"Li!"

As usual that day, Liwei had been away in the salt mines, employed in a low-level management job that made him despised by the miners, protected but also diminished by De's father. What Li didn't know was that De *had* heard her. De's father had phoned, the ring breaking the silence that had ensconced their morning. Removing cotton from one ear, her mother shooed De away to the courtyard to flick lit matches into the drain the way she and her brother had done when they were children, escaping their parents' fights. Even from the courtyard she could hear her mother's voice, how firm and unfamiliar it sounded to her, how much she wished, speaking fierce words or kind ones, that it was directed at her. As she listened, the fire caught. She watched the paper curtains go up so fast.

BIRDSONG BECAME A BACKDROP to Lila and James's daily lives which irritated Lila on days when she returned from work tired and seeking quietude. Lila no longer relied on her alarm but instead woke when the singing began, instigated by a singular distance-dimmed bird that swelled to a chorus awakening them both just before dawn.

James made a habit of leaving open his front door so he might see the woman. While he relished his isolation, he was curious to know more about her, the nature of her solitude, so tentative the two of them in their conditions, separated only by hallways and doors. But she did not emerge.

One morning, James rose and boiled two eggs, put the kettle on the burner and took the last two tea bags from the tin. He would knock on the woman's door today. He hoped to find her at home across the hall, expecting him somehow, familiar and strange all at once. James knocked gently on the door but when she did not come, he left her the boiled egg in a silver egg cup—the kind with the pedestal, from a set given to him and Lila by his mother-in-law as an engagement gift so many years ago, a gift he'd considered unnecessary until now.

De was watching *All My Children* when she heard the knock at her door and froze, waiting longer than she guessed most Americans thought it necessary to wait. Then, she quietly lifted her eye to the peephole and peered through. She opened the door and safely took in the egg, still warm in its shell. The thrushes eyed her suspiciously as she peeled it and cut the white with a spoon before smearing it on a piece of toast.

James awoke the next day and spent the morning researching birds. He learned of their respiratory systems, how they mimic the early predatory dinosaurs, their lungs a series of sacks that cycle air through chambers. He listened to their songs online, was hoping to guess which varieties the woman kept as he listened to them through two closed doors. He had promised Lila he'd devote an hour each day to apply for jobs, but he often spent no more than twelve minutes at the task, opting instead to dream of opening a used bookstore, some place a person wandered without objective but occasionally found something unexpected—a different happiness. He imagined their savings might cover a few month's rent on the corner shop in Inman Square that had become available a few weeks ago.

Most days, De stayed inside, the television on mute in the background, among the company of her birds that sang intermittently and sometimes in chorus, instigated by the mournful cry of the blue thrush. She watched soap operas exclusively now, first the American ones and then those which she could find on cable networks way up in the 900s. She marveled at the expressions of the men and women as they held each other, as they turned away, as they fled for the door. How dramatic and decided they were. How telling their faces looked. She had never seen her mother yield to emotion this way, and it made her more conscious of her own face, its revelations and mysteries. Now, as she watched, she retrieved a small handheld mirror from the bathroom and mimicked the face of the actress who sat on an exam table in a paper gown, conjuring tears.

AFTER A WEEK OF WAITING, James approached the woman's apartment door a second time. He listened to the bird songs within. He brought his hand up and struck the door. Only moments later, he heard the slide of the peephole. The door opened.

She stood in a swirl of dark clothes: a long skirt, black boots laced up beneath it, a black scarf coiled at her neck.

"My name is James," he said. "I live there." He pointed to the apartment across the hall.

"De," she said.

"Day? Your name is Day?"

She nodded, tentatively. It was only then that he was able to see past her to the cages in the apartment. The birds were silent.

Then, as if remembering suddenly, she disappeared for a moment and returned with the silver egg cup he'd left at her door.

"Thank you for the…" her accent was strong and she trailed off as if searching for the correct word.

James interrupted. "No problem. If there's anything you need, I'm home most of the time, and I wouldn't mind some company."

De nodded and shut the door.

When Lila returned from work, James's heart seemed to tick along so consciously he could count out six-minute intervals. He was preparing Bolognese, her favorite.

"The birds are quiet for once," Lila said as she joined him in the kitchen. The crease between her eyebrows was dark and persistent.

He listened. "They were singing all day."

"You should say something."

"It doesn't bother me. I kind of like it. When they first moved in, I saw her with the cages. There must've been a dozen."

"It's probably against some kind of health code, right?"

"Maybe. But they're pets. And they're always quiet when we're sleeping."

"You're the one who has to live with it most, I guess." Her face softened. James took her cheeks in his palms, smoothed the wrinkle between her eyes with his thumbs. She tried to relent, opened her mouth for a kiss, though her yielding had grown more complicated by her resentment. When they were in public, among other couples and lovers who seemed so captivated by one another's company, Lila would try whimsy. She would smile broadly, laugh out of place, chasing the excitement that seemed always just out of reach, the distance between the ideal and their love's present condition growing wider with time.

He kissed her then. They were alone: no on-lookers, benign or otherwise, to witness it. Their lips pressed together awkwardly, their breathing did not align. They withdrew from one another dissatisfied.

"We should have them for dinner some time." Lila blew on a steaming spoonful of sauce before tasting it. "Needs salt," she said.

"What would we cook?"

"I don't know. Bolognese. Whatever."

"What would me and the man talk about?"

"Why would it be different than having anyone else to dinner? Because they're Asian?"

"Because we don't know them. Because afterward, maybe we'll know more than we want to."

"James, it's just dinner."

When James and Lila sat down, it took them exactly twelve minutes from their first bite to clean plates. He didn't ask the neighbors to dinner.

The following day, when James left the apartment for the grocery store, the hallway smelled of sweet vinegar and oil. He heard the birds singing from inside the apartment. On the sidewalk outside, he looked up at her window, half open, which let the smells drift down and deliver themselves to him. De was working at the stove, a splash of yellow on her black shoulder. He stood on the street and hoped she might turn to see him. No luck.

When James returned to his apartment, his bags filled with rice, boneless spareribs, Napa cabbage and a neat, glass jar of plum sauce (an Americanized thirty-minute meal learned from Rachael Ray), he could not be sure of what he heard—a soft whirring from behind his apartment door like the sound of his own heartbeat in his ears. He opened the door in a rush and found his kitchen window wide open though he hadn't remembered leaving it that way. A yellow bird banged against a cabinet and then again off the glass pane before fleeing through the window.

At dinner, Lila devoured the pork and cabbage and helped herself to a second plate. "Hard at work again, my man of luxury?" She assumed frivolity was the byproduct of idle time. He told her he'd read about China, refamiliarized himself with the dynasties, learned of Duanwu, its legends and traditions.

"You're interested in China all of the sudden?" she asked.

"I realize I don't know anything about anywhere, really."

She nodded her head suspiciously, so he changed the subject, told her there was a voicemail from her mother.

"She called my cell. She wants to come for a visit. And I'd like her to stay with us, but…"

"You don't want me home all day?"

"She's resourceful," Lila said.

"I can take her to do things. We can meet you for lunch one day. And I can always go to the library and give her space," he said, clearing their plates.

"Well, Jobless James, how's the search going?"

"I thought you were okay with me taking some time off."

"I am. I'm just… how long do you think you'll need?"

"I'm not sure. I need to decide if I want to open something small—a private consulting business or if, um, I'm done with law. That corner store in Inman would be perfect for a little bookstore."

"Done with law? You didn't work your ass off and spend a fortune so you could dust books off with your shirt sleeves, James."

"But I can't spend my life logging billable hours every six minutes when I know what I'm doing is cheating someone of something. I thought I'd want it, but I don't want to make partner. I don't even know if I want to practice."

"Don't you want to buy a bigger place? Don't you want to travel? Improve our lives?" she said, throwing a disdainful glance in the direction of the birdsong that moments before had begun to sing in chorus. Now, a bird sang solo. It seemed to call to him.

Forming in James's imagination was the frailest vision of a life beyond this apartment, an improvement she might approve of, a blanket laid out on an expanse of spring-green lawn, two sweaty glasses on a tray, while he lay reading in the sun, waiting for his company to join him—a dark-haired woman who might've been Lila though he realized, uneasily, it was more likely De. It wasn't the possibility of De that surprised him, but that it might've been anyone other than Lila.

"Then figure it out!" she shouted, squashing the vision. "Get past this personal crisis. It's been two months. It's not working!"

In bed that night, after the birds went to sleep, they made love with the lights on. This was Lila's way of making up for saying things he wished she regretted. Lila often tipped her head away from him, let her brown hair fall to one side, revealed to him the fluttering of her neck as the pulse worked its way against the tender skin. It was the change in her breath that was her apology.

ONE MORNING WHILE JAMES was making tea, there was a knock at the door. He knew it was De without having to check the peephole. He invited her in, put a cup of tea in her hand, offered her a seat on the couch with the sweep of his hand. CNN was on in the background which relieved the pressure of attempting conversation.

Three weeks later, they spent most mornings this way, wordless in their routine, existing at convenient intersections. During the day, their apartments became extensions of one another's. James was often startled when he looked up from the newspaper after an hour, maybe more, to find her where she had not been before, looking at magazines, legs crossed on his sofa. Other times, he rose to reheat the kettle, called her name, expecting her to want a second cup of tea and found her absent. Her transience was startling—the way she descended on him and alighted.

When he slept, James dreamed De had tucked herself between him and Lila, her hair naturally black beneath a hat of yellow feathers, its veil pulled over her closed eyes. Her presence did not startle him. When he peeled back the covers, her body dissolved to feathers and dust. And Lila, too, was turned suddenly stone—a museum statue like one he'd seen, her gaze disappointed, her fingers blunt.

He didn't consider it a betrayal against Lila that he and De now drank tea most mornings, that he had learned how to slide air between his tongue and the roof of his mouth to say "thank you" in Chinese. James did not tell Lila that De had begun to bring him pictures of people in the newspaper saying, "What is this feeling…?" as she pointed at their expressions, wanting him to say the word in English that distinguished the shades of meaning in their faces. He didn't tell Lila that he'd seen photographs of De's young mother and father, or that that they sometimes spent afternoons watching soap operas on mute or that they fed pigeons in Central Square. Though there had been plenty of opportunities, he didn't tell Lila because he had intuited more about this woman in their silence than he had with his wife in all their years together.

Late one evening, Lila came home and announced she'd just met Mr. 3B on the stairs. Even after three months, James had only seen the man once, that first day, when he'd witnessed them arguing in the moving van.

"Seems like an okay guy," Lila said.

"Does he speak English?"

"As good as you and I—*and* he accepted my invitation to dinner."

"You invited them to dinner? When?"

"Friday night."

James had engaged in private speculation about De's life with her partner, and a formal meeting would complicate that invention. James hadn't wanted to imagine the ways the man loved De, if his hands still smelled of cooking oil when he touched the base of her neck before kissing her. James only wanted to imagine the man cruel, selfish, unfit to be her companion. Dinner might destroy that. James knew that when he and De's time came to an end (it was certain to, he admitted that, tentative as they were, nearly wordless in their companionship, their relationship patient and obscure), no desire, secret or otherwise, would keep him from enduring with Lila.

DE DID NOT KNOCK ON JAMES'S DOOR the day of the dinner, nor did he on hers. When he left the apartment to walk to the bakery on Broadway to buy a lemon tart, he could hear the commanding "sit-sit-sit" of De's Nutchatch louder than ever. James wondered what she had told her husband about how she spent her days—if she ever told him she had learned to distinguish more clearly the words for the emotions she groped for from *As the World Turns* and *All My Children*. That she had welcomed another man into her apartment and showed him her birds, sang to him their songs in a language as different from hers as it was from his. Regarding dinner, it wouldn't be guilt that James felt, even if the man wiped at his gracious mouth and nodded approvingly at the food. It wouldn't be shame. It would be something he couldn't yet name, like looking at a face in a foreign newspaper, the only correct word for the emotion in a language one does not speak.

THE KNOCK ON THE DOOR WAS synchronized with the hall clock's seven chimes. Lila opened the door to find the woman dangling a birdcage from her pointer finger. Inside was a small yellow bird, a species for which they would never learn the name, silently perched on its thin bar, its head jerking about like some wind-up toy. "For you," said the man as De extended it toward Lila.

"A bird?"

"They aren't too difficult to care for if you follow a few simple rules," said the man. "And this one is silent in our company."

Lila tried to smile and, holding the cage away from her body, led the two into the kitchen where James was cooking.

"Look, James," she said, carefully placing the cage on the counter. "Our guests have brought us a bird."

As if rescuing it, De removed the bird from its cage and sat with it in her hands, a subtle distraction from the air of embarrassment about her. She never looked directly at James, only nodded and smiled sheepishly at Lila. It made him nervous. They learned the man's name was Liwei and his English was very good. After a brief inquiry in bird-care, Lila made gin and tonics while James prepared dinner. They all sat casually on the barstools at the counter while Lila asked them polite questions about China. They learned the two had come to Boston so Liwei could take over a family restaurant in Chinatown, an establishment begun by his uncle. From time to time, Liwei turned to De and spoke in Mandarin, his face so placid it seemed bereft of emotion. She nodded and sometimes replied, her face going blank like his. James considered it a kind of humorless endurance, the result of failed desire.

"I pardon my sister," Liwei said. James's knife slipped. He looked at De whose eyes were cast down at the bird. "She speaks English, but hasn't much since the accident." James kept his eyes fixed on her, hoping for a glance, a twitch, something that might acknowledge this revelation. De had hardly spoken English with James; she had let on that she didn't know it. But more than that, she had not told James the man was her brother, and yet, it was James who had made the assumption.

"Accident?" asked Lila, "I'm sorry, that's terribly forward."

De did not look up.

"I would not mention it if I didn't care to explain." Liwei told them about their upbringing in Dafeng, a city a few hours from Shanghai. Their father had worked in salt production but bought a business on the side, capitalizing on the tourist interest in the nature preserves. He began collecting birds of all kinds, eventually buying a shop where his wife and daughter made handmade cages from bamboo and water reeds. In a flash, James remembered the man berating De the morning they moved into the apartment. He wanted him to be calculated and cruel.

"My sister watched the shop burn to the ground. Our mother was inside," Liwei said. De's voice plucked vigorously at her brother for a moment then fell silent again.

Lila looked at her, begging for a connection. "I'm so sorry. I can't imagine…"

De responded, narrowing her eyes. "My brother is suggesting I let her burn alive. When I tried the door, it was locked. Shut from the inside. She never cried out." It was the most fluid progression of English James had ever heard her speak.

Liwei pursed his lips. "Only De and some of the birds in the courtyard survived." James glanced at Lila and then back at De who sat motionless. He waited for Liwei to expose some small affection for his sister. If the man had reached for her hand, even if he hadn't found it possible to forgive her, it might've signaled compassion, it might have provided De and James, too, what one is always hoping for—to be surprised in the face of certain disappointment, to salvage hope from some small act of compassion.

"Dinner smells delicious," Liwei announced. Lila made a second round of drinks, this one stronger than the first. At dinner, they talked about the present, Liwei engaging with De from time to time, his voice rasping and ebbing, smooth then startling, unintelligible to James and Lila. James and Lila asked about the family business, where in Chinatown it was located, their specialties, Liwei's training.

"Do you have any other siblings?" James asked.

"No. It is rare to have two. My father needed help in the salt mines and De came first, so they had another. This time a boy."

"It's good you have each other." James said, though his voice rose so precipitously at the end of the question it admitted condescension. Lila concentrated on her food and moved her hand under the table to scold James with a squeeze of the thigh. Liwei seemed unmoved by James's comment: too proud or too inexperienced with the nuance of American intonation. De finally met his gaze, her eyes apologetic. The yellow bird jerked its neck and adjusted its feet on the perch.

"SHE SEEMS SO CONSTRAINED," Lila said as they washed the dishes afterwards.

"It's him."

"Or it's her."

"He's her brother!" James said, tossing a spoon into the drying rack.

"Why does that surprise you?"

"I thought they were together. Married."

"What difference would it make?" Lila asked.

It would mean that desire and intent, his and hers alike, had been tempered by fictions, by assumptions, and by what James could not help but feel was a dishonest exertion of De's power. And now, knowing they were siblings would make no less startling her presence in his life, her movement among the rooms, but it made her silence not only a falsity but a manipulation. It meant she was deceptive.

"The fire. She didn't go back for her mother? Or she couldn't get her out?" Lila asked.

James didn't respond. He was most unsettled by not knowing De's potential.

"How terrible." Lila placed the last plate in the cupboard and went to the bird cage which rested on the table. "What are we going to do about this bird?" she said. It seemed to be evaluating them, its neck ticking back and forth between them.

"I don't know much about birds, but I think it needs a bigger cage," James said.

"Why would they think bringing a bird as a gift would be a good idea? I wouldn't bring someone a puppy."

James shrugged and approached the cage. "It needs a name." The bird twitched ambivalently. "What kind of bird are you?" James asked.

"A yellow one," Lila said.

"I could ask De." James smirked to belie what felt only like betrayal.

"She's quite beautiful don't you think? Even with that weird copper-colored hair."

James confessed with a nod.

"She likes you," she said.

"She hardly looked at me."

"Playing hard to get, maybe." Lila smacked her soapy hand against James's rear end. He was startled by her levity, and it made his heart ache. The bird sputtered into song, like a hoarse but persistent siren. The couple was transfixed. Now, it grew bolder, loud and laser-like. It sang this way until they turned off the kitchen lights and retreated to the bedroom.

"I thought the man said it didn't sing," she whispered as they lay in the dark.

"No, he said it was silent in *their* company."

"Oh."

In the darkness, a subtle happiness crept in so quietly, James didn't know it was there.

THE NEXT DAY, JAMES WANTED to walk to the pet store in the square to buy a bigger cage for the bird. On his way out, he knocked on De's door. She opened it as if she'd been waiting on the other side expectantly. Her eyes were cast down.

"Look at me," James said.

She raised her face to him. After weeks of silence and the sharing of rooms, assuming their silence was more eloquent than rough language and misunderstanding, all he wanted was to know her intent.

"Did you intend to deceive me?"

De fixed him with her stare.

"Did you?" he continued. But, no words came from her lips. "And?" Now he shook his head, more at his foolishness than at her deceit, "He's your brother?"

"Yes."

She was changing before him—becoming a slow wind that blew coolly through him. "I'm walking to the square.

The bird needs a bigger cage," he said, and turned down the hallway. The previous evening's revelations gnawed at him.

De slid on shoes and ran after him. She caught up within the block, syncing her pace to his but saying nothing. The terms of their silence were revising themselves. Now, silence could not repair them, could not draw them back to a time before they'd failed each other. They were nearly to the square when she finally spoke.

"I don't speak because I don't want to."

"But you can. And now we have a relationship complicated with lies."

"What lies?"

"You let me think you didn't know how to speak English. You let me think Liwei was your husband!"

"That is your own doing."

"You said nothing of your mother's death!"

They sat on a bench facing the street, watching the pigeons congregate near black puddles. "I didn't tell you about Dafeng, about the fire and my mother because I don't know how to describe my emotions. My father is not a good man. My mother spent her life trying to please him."

Feeling his anger suddenly misdirected, he said, "I'm sorry."

"It turned her to stone. She grew silent and her silence controlled everything. It controlled me."

"And *your* silence controlled me?" he asked sharply.

"You didn't enjoy our silence?"

"I did—but I liked it because I didn't know it could be any different. I feel like a fool."

"Because you were presumptuous?" Her eyes pierced him.

"You *let* me expect something else of you." He was thinking of the day she first opened the door to his introduction, and formed the syllables in her mouth as if she were discovering them for the first time.

"Don't confuse your own desire with reality. Let me remind you, you have a wife." Her words were keen and fierce. "My silence liberated you."

"Excuse me?"

"That's what we do. We imagine ourselves into other things. All those years I spent in silence beside my stoic mother, both of us were wishing ourselves out." Her eyes traveled over the square. "Maybe the fire freed her."

"But not you?"

She shrugged, an American gesture signaling indifference or uncertainty, though he could tell she was neither.

"You've begun to wonder about the life you chose, right?" she asked.

James considered the question.

She continued, "Silence lets you re-imagine the possibilities."

JAMES PICKED LILA'S MOTHER up at Logan Airport on a Thursday morning, which meant he had two whole days to entertain her, accommodate and avoid her as needed until the weekend when Lila would take over. He and Connie had never grown close, having reached a level of comfort during his and Lila's first year of marriage that had sustained them enough to get along without knowing each other too intimately. Still, James sensed she thought him selfish, disapproved of the dreamer in him, thought ideas that risked economic stability were selfish. Having not visited in years, perhaps her arrival was an indictment of his recent unemployment.

In the evenings during Connie's visit, James poured the ladies glasses of wine while they chatted in the living room, then he retreated to the kitchen to prepare dinner. Initially, Lila had felt irritated by the presence of the bird, thinking it a constant voyeur, but by this time she had grown fond of it, taking it from the cage within minutes of arriving home each evening. Lila had even brought home a wheeled dolly from school so that she could move the bird about the different rooms of the apartment. James was unsure if she did this so that the bird could bear witness or because Lila worried about it being alone. Even her mother could not dissuade her from its affection.

"It was a gift," she explained that evening, as she allowed the bird to eat cracker crumbs from her hand.

Her mother adjusted her position on the couch. "What an odd gift."

"Our neighbors gave it to us. Their parents owned a bird shop when they lived in China."

"Oh. You have Chinese neighbors?"

"I like the bird now. At first, I thought it was a burden. But, it's really quite affectionate toward James and me."

Then Lila called to James from the couch, wanting to prove to her mother its dearness. James appeared in the doorway. Lila knew her mother's feelings towards James, and, challenging her on issues mostly having to do with love, she beckoned to him with her free hand.

"Watch this," she said to her mother as the bird continued its pecking.

James leaned in to kiss Lila on the cheek while Connie watched.

The bird remained silent.

Lila took hold of James's neck and pulled him to her lips. The muscles in his neck flexed. It would be more embarrassing to resist his wife than have his mother-in-law witness an act of affection. Their lips met.

Again, the bird remained silent.

"That's funny. It usually begins to sing when it sees us showing affection," said Lila. "Our neighbor said it was a silent bird when they had it, but for us, it sings like crazy."

"Stage fright?" suggested James, annoyed with his wife.

All evening, the bird remained silent even as Lila repeatedly advanced on James. As he cooked, she drew her arms around his waist from behind. At dinner, she draped a bare arm across his shoulder from such an angle that it was both uncomfortable and awkward. When Connie excused herself to the bathroom, James whispered, "Cut it out, Lila. This is embarrassing."

"Showing affection's embarrassing?"

"No, but you're putting on a show."

"The bird's not responding."

"So?"

"So, something's wrong."

"Nothing's wrong except that I feel pressured by my wife and embarrassed in front of my mother-in-law."

The following morning, James was clearing Connie's dishes when a knock came to the door. Even before James could approach it, the doorknob was turning. Connie stood abruptly, dusting the toast crumbs from her lap. There was De in her pajama pants and tank top which, now because of the mother-in-law's presence, seemed indecent.

"Oh," the women both said simultaneously—De, in a tone not startled nor regretful and Connie as if punctuated with a question mark.

"Connie, this is our neighbor De. De, Connie, my mother-in-law."

"Pleasure," replied Connie, nodding her head suspiciously.

"I'm sorry. I didn't know you had company," said De, looking down at her choice of apparel.

"You're the neighbor who gave my daughter the bird."

"I am, yes."

De looked at James then, as if requesting a cue. That's when it began to sing. The bird had been silent all morning, silent for days. Even as James felt guilty for being so tense, so annoyed with his wife for the previous evening's behavior that he pursued her in return this morning, pushing her hair back to kiss her cheek as she came to retrieve a second cup of coffee. It had been in plain view of the bird, surely it had seen them, and yet it made no sound. Lila had sighed, a final surrender to their failed efforts and turned toward the door to leave for work. But now, now the bird was singing as James and De stood there searching each other's faces.

"Well," sighed Connie. "It sings." De smiled and covered her mouth. "And isn't it a charming tune?"

"I should be going," said De.

She retreated as quickly as she had come.

OVER THE NEXT FEW WEEKS, De commanded him. "What is …" and then as if conscious but not regretful of the misconception she had created in James's mind, she would continue: "…the English word for this emotion?" She showed him a newspaper photo of a woman brought to her knees as she held a limp child. She pointed not to the subject but to a woman looking on in the background, her face out of focus, her mouth open, aghast and helpless.

Looking up from his own reading, James replied, "Grief? Something like grief?" But that wasn't it.

"Bey," she said—a sound so short James didn't know if he'd heard the first consonant correctly. Then, she erupted. "Why do you say 'something like grief?' Is it or is it *not* grief?" she demanded, startling him, shaking him even further away from her. It was her urgency that he could not understand, her new impatience that suddenly made him at her behest. The bird, who's cage was open, ceased pecking its cuttlebone, ticked its head into position and stared at him.

Now, pointing at the photograph he said, "I cannot know her emotion, the way I cannot know you." He was exhausted by her.

Now the bird alighted, flying from its cage to hover between them, suspended in silence as if to show off its yellow, its audacity, its skill at diversion. Suddenly, the bird dipped its head and beat its wings and was off, flitting around the kitchen manically before it glided through the bedroom door and landed on the headboard. There, it began its serenade. First a song for De: creeping, seductive notes that slid through the air longingly. De followed it to the bed without permission, the bird retreating as she moved toward it. Now, she skirted to the opposite side of the bed, her arms outstretched to capture it. It was when James appeared in the door that a new song began: steady notes that up-ticked and faltered, the bird's head once again jerking steadily between them. James was hoping it would cooperate, that she would catch it and bring it back to the living room, out of the place of couples and promises and secrets and intimacy. But the bird fluttered above the bed, seemed to hover there, like a small yellow helicopter, coming to rest alternately on the footboard and headboard. De began plucking at the bird in Mandarin the way she had at Liwei the night of the dinner. The bird would not obey. When she reached for it, it flew through her hands and landed on James's shoulder, taunting her. James strained his head away from the bird uneasily. She was angry now, her face cool and rigid with frustration as she crept slowly across the bed toward James to collect it.

In his dreams, De had laid where her knees were pressing into the mattress. He dreamed she let him touch her face, an intimacy greater than most. Now, she coaxed the bird into one hand. The two were there in silence, in the place of shadows and dreams, the bird their only witness. James could have chased his temptation, appeased any lingering curiosity, or killed it on the spot. That De was sister, not wife, changed nothing now. He did not want to lie with her, did not want to imagine her black raven hair on his pillow. He couldn't yet conjure what he would say to the woman to make her a stranger again. He did not yet know what avoidance would look like, nor truths nor lies, nor what he would tell his wife.

That's when he heard the key inserting in the lock, De and James's heads turning toward the sound in syncopation. How many minutes had passed? Lila was home. Early? The bird song persisted. De turned her face squarely to James as she held the bird tight to quiet it. The bolt dropped and the front door creaked open. James felt his face seize in fear, the muscles in his forehead contract. He drew a breath coolly against the roof of his mouth. The bird wanted to sing, to announce the relationship, their place in the bedroom together. De closed her grip on the bird. James was paralyzed, he wanted to turn to feathers and dust. Lila was approaching in the hall saying, "James? James?" The bird struggled to sing, its vocal chords buzzing against the flesh of De's thumb. James's gaze went cold in De's. Her eyes sparked and died. In one swift motion, De twisted the bird's neck, like turning a key in a lock and whispered, "Second chance." The bird went silent, limp.

James could not yet know the name for this emotion, nor for the look in her resin eyes when she rolled off the bed and out of view. He could not yet know the nature of forgiveness and compromise or that when he woke from dreams, and let his eyes adjust in the dark, he could hear the bird even as he groped for his wife's body in a tangle of cool sheets. What James could not know was that in De's absence, there would not be longing but more emptiness, the kind that occurs when a flock of pigeons sucks the air from a courtyard as it takes flight. He could not yet know, even as he touched her, how much he would wish to have her back.

C3PGirl

All across Egrette, fathers, mothers, daughters, and sons answer doorbells, pin corsages, smile into cameras. Once her date arrives, Cece Neely and Harold Murphy might be any other couple on their way to the prom. She cannot tell her father now, his camera pulsing away, the mess of silver tubes and gears rising above the top of her blue tulle dress, he regarding her courage as the ultimate sign of her recovery, that her attendance at the prom is not as much a choice as a necessity.

    Cece's father directs her to stand beneath the elm tree in front of the house, where the light filters gently through the leaves in such a way that the reflection from her exposed silver-socket shoulders doesn't disturb the camera's white balance. Her father has already made a place for the photograph he'll hang in the foyer family gallery next to pictures of Cece's mom and dad in faraway places, like Utah and North Dakota, where the landscape is like that of an undiscovered planet. Her parents stand among vast landscapes: red boulders or sand, their flesh and blood emphasized by the expanse of cliff, shore and rock. Cece has allowed her father to hang only a few photos in which she is featured—those in which her body, even while hidden beneath long-sleeved clothing and thick sweaters, remains concealed by the family dog or the more confident bodies of others.

Now the white van, property of Holden Place Rest Home, cruises slowly down their street. Murph is at the wheel, hands at ten and two. Cece watches the old man intently, watches him salute hello, watches the direction of his gaze and is surprised to find it trained on the road—dutiful, undistracted by the exhibition of gears, metal, and joints glinting in the sun. Cece expects him to inventory her corporeal machinery, to make sense of the explanation she'd once provided him (a lie). But instead, Murph steps out of the van to shake her father's hand, a man lock step with chivalry even as it dies. Then, he turns to his date for the evening, looks first at her flawless, powdered face, turns his lips into a complacent frown and asks, "So this is it, huh?"

This was it: what she was left with after the storm took her mother. Their arms hooked at the elbows, they'd gone out to the hill above the lake to watch the lightning as it lashed wildly at earth and water, then tree and mother. Her father lost his wife and she lost her own flesh and bones that were not yet those of a woman. When she finally returned home from the hospital, the tragedy banged around inside her long after her scars healed, long after she figured how to hide it all, even long after Cece began her father-mandated company-keeping arrangement with Harold Murphy.

Murph straightens his red knit tie and inspects the front of his suit jacket. And since everyone wants to touch her, everyone wants to know exactly in which way and in which parts Cece Neely is robot or girl, she takes the opportunity to make contact with Murph—to hook her arm through his. He doesn't flinch or recoil even as his elbow discovers the steel cage of her ribs. Just the image of this steel cage might be enough to inspire beautiful, popular girls to sink deep into the chests of their beautiful, popular boyfriends and ache for a ruined, pretty girl, her heart caged in wire. That's why she plasters on a big, electrifying smile, the kind that deflects pity, and leans into her date. This is the photograph her father will hang in the foyer.

Most of the cars and limos in Egrette High's parking lot this evening will be tricked out with blue lights and polished rims. But Cece and Murph cruise in a white van, property of Holden Place Rest Home, with handicapped access, a mechanical lift and a legit hang tag so they can park close.

"Nice ride," Cece says. She figures if she's gonna do this thing, she might as well go full tilt.

"It was this or Art's Buick."

"Good choice. Hydraulics score major points with the popular set," she smirks.

On the highway, her eyes skim across the roofs of cars and through the diaphanous exhaust to the Tastee-Dip and the Golden Corral and the rest of the steel, plastic and concrete feed-lots laid thick beneath the dusky May sky. Steel and solder can make a building so sturdy that it might never collapse, and the bones of a girl who just might.

"That color is nice on you," Murph says, never glancing in her direction.

She'd prefer the dignity of questions to compliments. *What does it feel like?* Go ahead, touch it. *How did they do it?* Thirteen hours, three surgeons, a sculptor from Manhattan. *Blood or oil?* Blood on the inside, oil in the joints. If only Murph would ask questions, provide her one glimmer of fearlessness to prepare her for the evening, she might be able to lead confidently, draw into her iron lungs the fullness of a proud breath because she's got you now, suckers. But Murph asks nothing. Maybe this is the subtlety gained in old age. Maybe he is showing her how to get what you want without giving away how much you want it.

Except for her father, no one has ever seen the way the metal clavicle hinges with the gears of her shoulder socket, the way the edges of her skin, where flesh ends and machine begins, are capped under neat metal disks so that everything is tidy and tolerable, no ragged, tender edges, no shiny purple scars—an artist's work and a surgeon's. Cece Neely—*Robogirl*, modern medical marvel, teenager on crash course with social judgment—is revealed.

She inventories Murph's van. It's been freshly vacuumed, a new pine tree air freshener looped on the rearview mirror. The bucket seat is raised so high her feet barely touch the mats. She flicks open the glove compartment, lifts the service manual, rifles through the registration, the Handi Wipes, the motion distress bag.

"So, this isn't a whiskey Saturday?" she asks, defeated.

"You kidding me? I've got precious cargo."

"Precious. Ha."

He shoots her a sidelong glance. "I'm serious. No chance I'd be drinking tonight."

Cece sighs.

"Plus, whiskey's for Fridays," he smiles.

IT WASN'T UNTIL THE THIRD MONTH of her "internship" at Holden Place that the whiskey had been introduced. Cece navigated her way through the corridors toward Murph's apartment, watching couples pull one another along while others slumped like statues (Still Life with Walker) on couch-oases halfway between here and the hereafter. When she reached his door, she heard whimpering from within and, entering, found him lying in the bed, a woman's framed photograph on the pillow beside him, a long yellow nightgown laid out where her body should have been. He sat up to blow his nose in his bed sheet. Cece stood there hoping he'd cue the appropriate reaction. Should she hug him? Murmur condolence? Back away? But instead, he got up and withdrew two short tumblers from the cabinet and poured himself a drink. He pretended to pour one for Cece, too, saying, "This is what the Irish do when they shoot the shit."

He took a sip and said, "Even if you know it's coming, you can't prepare." And then it was like something clamped down on his heart. "Gloria. She was it. She was everything." He leaned back, exhaling those words into a bubble above his head that grew and filled the room becoming, suddenly leaden, so heavy it threatened to crush the two of them, flatten the TV table and the bottle of Jameson. Murph began to wince and Cece was desperate to find a way to burst that bubble.

"You wanna see?" she'd said.

"See what?"

"You know…my robot parts."

He shook his head, disturbed.

"Yeah you do. Everyone wants to."

"I don't." Then he looked sickened. "I guess I'd be satisfied to know why."

Eventually, everyone asks why. She didn't want to lie to Murph, but it was easier than enduring the truth. She could've told him the conjoined twins rendition, the alien abduction rendition, but for Murph, she chose the drama of a shark attack. While she unwound the details of the tragedy, he looked into his lap, refusing her lies. She touched his hand. He withdrew it so quickly, as if startled from a dream and said, "I didn't mean why is your *body* like this. I want to know why you're so impossible."

"THIS COULD BE A MISTAKE," she says to the window now, a sudden pang of anticipated regret catching in the gears of her heart. When they arrive, there will be communal troughs of lukewarm Swedish meatballs and dancing in the café-gym-atorium under rigged disco lighting. When she makes her entry, the students' eyes will go wide, mouths will gape, they will be stunned—even the teachers' faces will betray any display of decency they formerly faked. And once they have judged her, they will turn to judge him. They will wonder about the old man in the new suit, they will point fingers at his knit tie and bare their ugly teeth.

"You don't want to go?" he asks.

"I don't know."

"Come on. I won the bet, remember?"

"You did. But it's a joke."

"I'll be damned."

Out of the corner of her eye, she considers his attire. His shoes are gleaming and his suit looks new, though the tie is out of season by years, eras. Cece had expected, though perhaps she should have suggested, that he might have dusted off something from his youth, something ruffled and ill-fitting, something out of tune enough to lend camp to their joke. He is too much in earnest. His silver hair is freshly cut and his beard is shaved close (the way a barber shop might with a straight edge) and he smells of Lilac Vegetal.

"Murph—you know this is all a joke," she says urgently now.

"If it's a joke then it'll be funny when we get there."

THE NIGHT THEY HAD BECOME prom dates had been another Whiskey Friday. Cece had explained to the old widower that during second period that day, Ms. Rios, the school social worker, told her if she *made more of a social effort, you know, try not to beat all of the boys in gym class*, she might have more friends. This from a woman who makes so much of a social effort herself that Principal Pliska left his wife of twenty-five years so he can stick his wiener in her on lunch break. So, Cece told Ms. Rios to shove it, and Principal Pliska reeled about respect and decency and the perils of bitterness. When he calmed down, he threatened to revoke senior prom privileges.

"Good story," Murph had said. "So, is Ms. Rios right?"

"No, she's not right. I don't *try* to beat the boys."

"So what's really eatin' ya, Cece?" he had said, calling her bluff.

She took an imaginary sip while Murph poured himself another glass. "How 'bout we started a new unit in PE this week—swimming."

"What, you rusty at swimming?" He winked. They clinked glasses and drank.

"It's even worse to watch and play towel girl from the bench while Randy Morris in his Speedo makes swoon-bags of all the bitches."

"But not you?" he teased.

"I've got swoon-bag immunity," Cece hammed, even though Randy Morris makes her want to vomit the contents of her titanium-lined stomach.

Since she had been vulnerable and Murph had been listening, she told him the story, true that time: During first period PE she'd watched the lap hand sweep the dial of the big clock and Randy Morris cut through the pool as if he were a fishing lure, the girls all wide-mouthed bass. The soles of his feet flashed and his shoulder blades skimmed the surface and his bathing-cap clad admirers gaped and cheered and jiggled their half-moon buns and breasts as Randy tried to beat another school freestyle record. When it was over, Cece's job was to hand him a towel, record his time, and try to appear as if she weren't in love. And since he'd acknowledged her in the past only in relation to how jealous he was that she outlasted him in just about any sport requiring impressive lung capacity, he jerked the towel from her hand and said, "Beat that, C3PGirl."

"What? A mechanical heart can't love?" Murph asked.

"High school love is bullshit. I mean, I'm sure you *looooved* Gloria. Old people can love like that—teenagers can't. Especially when Speedos have anything to do with it."

"We sure can. Barbara Brubaker in unit 101 has so much love left in her that men line up for it." He sipped. "Oh lighten up, Cece."

"Okay, so take the prom, right? The theme this year is *Sea of Love*. Could it get any more lame?"

Murph had put his hand over her empty glass and said, "The whiskey's making you mean, Ms. Cece. I'm gonna have to cut you off." Still, she remained unbudgingly straight-faced. "Gimme a break, kid. Why do you have to be so angry about a prom?"

"Because it's so stupid."

"Kids are stupid." He smiled. "So who's your date?"

"See? Stupid questions like that."

Murph shrugged his shoulders innocently and finished his second drink. "I might say you're missing an opportunity."

"For what?"

"To dance with greatness, Ms. Cece."

"Randy Morris won't dance with me anyway."

"Aha! Randy Morris." Murph was victorious.

"He's not my date, Murph. He's taking Alicia Marlow."

"I was classically trained, you know."

"In what? Catholic school pranks?"

"No. I took dance lessons from Gene Kelly."

"Who's that?"

"*Singin' in the Rain*?"

"You've got a story for everything," she said, rolling her eyes.

He moved his drink aside. "Let me show you. If I can dance, you let me be your date. If I can't dance, you sit here and stew about it. Deal?"

She shook the old man's hand.

That's how the two end up driving this van on the highway headed west toward Egrette High, with the windows down and the radio playing the musak version of *Blame it on the Rain*, and Cece ready to serve up the cold answer to Egrette High's questions with the help of a man who has never asked one. She wants the joke to be on the girls with perfect cleavage and on the boyfriends they will marry, on

Principal Pliska and Ms. Rios and every teacher who has ever pitied her, judged her, instructed her in how to behave. Cece clasps her hands over her mechanical heart where the rush and suck of it has risen to audible levels.

"Nervous?" Murph asks.

She tries in vain to muffle the sound. "Stupid heart."

She notices a photo tucked in to the flap of his sun visor. "May I?" she asks, pulling the photo from its place. It's not a studio shot, the kind that embalms the subject in a flawless mist. It's a close-up of Gloria standing in a tomato garden. Her green eyes shine out from the shadow of a large yellow sun hat, the fruit so big and beautiful they crowd her.

"What would Gloria say?" Cece asks.

"To me? 'Save a dance for me.' To you?" He pauses.

Cece turns to him now and sees it accidentally: Murph engaged in the invention of Gloria, memory pushing itself on him like rapture.

"What? What would she have said?" Cece asks again.

"I don't know," he replies, though she can tell he does know. And then he says, "Do you know you're beautiful?"

And it doesn't matter now if those are Gloria's words or his. She cannot be beautiful. "What's your favorite part? The gears, the joints, the bars, the brackets?"

"The fact that I can see it," he answers.

"Well, then, Mr. Murphy, you're just like all of the boys," she teases, "You wanna see what's in my pants." Cece slaps her thigh.

"Is that what they want?"

Her eyes float in a film of tears. "They want to see what a freak looks like."

He brings the van to a stop among a steady stream of Hummers, limos and borrowed cars slowly progressing toward Egrette High's café-gym-atorium.

"We don't have to go," Murph says.

She shakes her head and clears away the suggestion. The drivers behind them honk their horns. The orange-vested security guard wildly waves his lighted baton. Murph finally veers into a handicapped parking space. He cuts the engine and hands her a handkerchief. Cece dabs at her eyes and checks her make-up again in the visor mirror, angling it so that she can see down the top of her strapless dress, through the network of silver bars and tubes to where a heart of tissue and muscle should be sinking.

"Ready?" he asks.

Her wrist corsage is the weight of a dinner plate as they cross the parking lot. Through the glass, she can see Principal Pliska and Ms. Rios taking tickets and marking down arrival times in the manner of their usual fastidious record-keeping. She can see the photographer and the line of couples preening as they await their photo opp. That's when she imagines her heart seizing like an engine—a mass of unmaintained gears and pistons grinding to a halt. Murph places the confident mass of his hand at her back, where machine ends and flesh begins. He urges her forward. "May I?" he asks, sweeping open the door, the sound of music and chatter lapping toward them.

The lobby is hung with nets and heart shaped balloons and a banner that reads, *Dive into the Sea of Love*. Beyond reception, the heavy wooden doors to the gym open and shut revealing flashes of colored light, skin, taffeta, and shiny hair. Ms. Rios's mouth finally stops moving. Her lips slacken and gape while Principal Pliska's twitch into the hyper-assured grin of feigned approval.

"Hello, Cecelia. Who have you brought as your guest?"

"This is Mr. Harold Murphy," Cece announces.

It's Rios, trained in sensitivity, whose shock overcomes her. She stares at Cece's shiny shoulders as she records their names, never looking down to see the p-h-y spilling off the form and onto the desk.

Now, every eye in the lobby is transfixed by the revealed steel of her torso: Coach Willard, Mrs. Henley, the librarian,

Jenny Lewis, and Ralph Mandello who always treated her with decency. They do not—*can* not—conceal their horror. Their mouths and eyes make shapes she has not seen before. Silence floods her ears. She is underwater in the dark sea of love. Murph smiles and mouths something at her while he takes her hand. She grips it tightly, urgently, but not like a vice, no, with tenderness. Murph guides her to the "x" on the floor in front of the faux aquarium. The photographer turns from Jenny and Ralph, his expectation of the new couple dissolving to horror, his thumb misfiring on the flash button to explode the room in light that gleams and then dies on Cece's body. They move quickly through the gym doors, open, shut, open, shut and into the swirling sea of love.

Like a wave, one by one, Cece is revealed to them. Margot Sandell's jaw drops. A boy in a red cummerbund draws close his date, covers her eyes. Blue light pulses on the panorama of faces caught in a crush of emotion: gasping, laughing, turning away. A black vested server holds his empty tray like a shield. A meatball drops from Liz Bower's fork and rolls down her white dress. Even the ones that scream are silent in her ears. Silence is the sound of myth come undone.

It's then that Cece takes the lead. She feels her own small, human bones inside Murph's hand as she pulls him through the sea of people to the edge of the dance floor where students sway, safe from scorn and embarrassment, where their reputations cannot be choked away from them. She releases his hand, places her palm firmly on his chest as if to push him away; *No I am not beautiful.* Cece takes short, quick breaths and dances herself to the center of the floor, her reflection sparking up its surface like heat rising from the road. Sound returns to her ears. Her heart does not know how to sink nor does it know how to swell. It bangs. Her shoulders twist and grind and glint in the light. She is both a spectacle and a symbol. A sham and a smash. She cannot allow the old man to join her. The sea is too deep.

farm. They'll remember Chew Turner, too. But maybe no one but me will remember Sal.

My older brother, Wes, calls every year to wish my son, Ben, a happy birthday and realizes just then that he's missed mine by two days. But it's not embarrassment that makes him talk to fill all the empty spaces in our conversation: "So how was it, Grant? Your birthday, I mean? Some good family time, huh? You must have had a cake and all that? Geez, two days earlier and Ben would have your same birthday." Some people are just quieter than others. He thinks I'm quiet to seem smarter or more controlled, but that's not the reason. I think people who talk less do so because of the memories they've accumulated—the ones struggling to consciousness like distance-dimmed stars coming through the haze of city lights.

This morning, in the Hallmark store, as I waited for the woman to fill thirteen balloons with helium, a memory surfaced. Just like that. And when she turned to me, I had the look of it on me, I'm sure I did. My eyes pinch at the corners, so my crow's feet deepen, and maybe I look skeptical or puzzled or pained. The woman was frightened for a moment, wondering if maybe I was having a stroke, or if I'd forgotten where I was or what I'd come for.

"Sir, your balloons," she said, as I tried to pull myself from the vision of Sal's blue BMX loaded in the back of Chew's truck, just before sunrise, not light enough yet for a reflection—just the dull, blue-gray veil of morning on everything. Now, all I can think of is how I'd gotten there too late, the wheels of his bike no longer moving freely through the frame the way they'd been known to do for hours with the help of even the slightest breeze. Just the wheels—dead still.

"Sir, your balloons," she said again.

I'M DRIVING BEN TO HIS BIRTHDAY PARTY at the paintball course in Camden. He is contemplative, a small V between

The Unseen

The local paper reports that Chew Turner, the farmer my father hired to grow alfalfa in the forty acres he owns out west of town, a man who tipped his hat and called my mother ma'am and only stepped inside if my father was home, has been indicted on three counts of child molestation and pornography. The article explains that three victims have come forward; one of the men is my age. But I don't read the article when it falls out of the birthday card from my mother, who sends eerie whispers from home in the form of news clippings. Instead, I let my eyes go fuzzy, like they do when I'm distracted, and read it near midnight, when I think my son and everyone is sleeping under night's heavy hand.

Days later, on the phone, my mother will ask me if I knew those boys. And I will say I remember their names, not their faces. I'll already be thinking about the boy the article doesn't name. My mother will say she sees Chew around town all the time: in the Shop Rite, whizzing past her on Route 15, at the high school football games. Like since she's read about him in the paper, he's multiplied. That's the consciousness of a small town. People notice each other out of duty and talk about it too, as if they might disappear if they don't. They remember every drowning in the Susquehanna, they remember the boy who took his life in the high school bathroom, the hate-filled arsonists who burnt the Amish his eyebrows that makes him look older than thirteen, as he stares at the industrial landscape through his window. The buildings are boxy and pragmatic and have a certain monotony to them the way the corn and soybean fields did where I was raised, ordered and managed as they were in neat rows and acres. Ben doesn't like to go there to visit anymore. He claims there's nothing to do in central Pennsylvania even though his grandparents have a game room, a Wii, and a stable full of horses. I want him to like it because I am born of that place. I am part of its memory, and its memory is mine.

Last summer when we visited, we fed the new ponies sugar cubes and flew kites, and I made a big deal of teaching him to fly fish—got him a vest and rod. He frowned the whole time and seemed miserable in his waders, swatting the bugs away from his face. I explained it takes a long time for a person to learn how to flick his wrists correctly, that part of fishing was patience and endurance and that every year he'd get a little bit better.

"Is it good so far? Your birthday, I mean?" I ask Ben.

He hums out the sound pattern of *I don't know* and his eyes remain fixed outside. I have grown tired of waiting for him to smile and talk to me.

"Kind of a crappy day," I say. "Good thing the course is inside."

"Good thing," he says.

He's been spending more time in his room than usual, reading graphic novels in silence, building model planes, stewing. His mother says he's got all the clinical signs after she reads a Newsweek article about adolescent depression in America. Last week, she lightly knocked on his door hoping to check what she calls his *emotional pulse*. I strained at the door to hear their conversation and when Shelly emerged reporting, "40 excruciating beats per minute," I could not bring myself to ask about the content of their conversation. Well-adjusted men know how to reveal themselves, and to whom at the appropriate time. I wonder about boys with the capacity for self-containment and what their chances are of being well-adjusted men.

"That F-14 model Grandpa got you looks like a challenge. We can try to do part of it together tomorrow if you want."

"I've done that kind before. It's not that hard. You just have to be careful you don't use too much cement or you can see it in the joints."

"Oh," I say. "Well, you're working on quite the collection. I'll have to build another shelf for your room."

"Okay, Dad." He's throwing me a bone. I'm being appeased by my thirteen-year-old son. I stop talking altogether for a while so that against the patter of rain on the window, the double-edged quiet settles around us. Right now, I am relieved he does not want to talk. He switches on the radio and scans to a channel that's all crashing and screaming. Then he sits back again and nods his head hyper-fast. I try, in vain, to decode the angry vocals.

"Do you know this song?" I say lightly. Condemning him would only deepen the chasm of disconnect.

"Not all of it. But I know the band," he says.

I should seize the opportunity to ask, but I can't. It's rattling my brain. "I can't even tell what they're saying. Do you listen to this kind of music a lot?"

"Bret listens to it."

Oh god, I think. His best pal listens to kill-your-mother music.

"I don't like it." But now I've done what I feared. It's just that it's so angry and dark and maniacal. I try to retrace my misstep, "I don't like that *you* like it. But you *can*."

My permission fails. Ben turns off the radio, pulls his Phillies cap low over his eyes and sulks. He hates me in ways I never imagined he might. He is my flesh and blood but in his mind, I am too old and far away and he would never guess that I had been angry and uncertain of so many things, too. I think about the news article again. The two men my age still live in central PA: one a prison guard, the other a college professor. I found their faces in my senior yearbook and now they were in my mind like Sal was, like ghosts. I wondered if I didn't know them then because of what Chew took from them that made them impossible to know.

THE SUMMER MY PARENTS CONSIDERED moving from Mount Joy to Japan so my father could teach and finish his book, we sold the house and lived in a rental on a small street by the Agway. To our left was a poorly kept apartment complex with peeling paint and food-stamp families, the presence of which my mother found insulting to her station in life. To our right were the neighbors who sold radiators in their yard. Who knew so many people had the need to dispense or reclaim old radiators? To add to her complaints, our rental was painted school bus yellow, its oven was crooked and the basement flooded regularly. But I loved it. Eight kids on the block made it easy to field a kickball team or play jailbreak. The alley was narrow and lit by streetlamps that Wes used to kick into submission by throwing his full weight against the base of the poles to make it dark enough for spin the bottle or flashlight tag. I got the sense that anything could happen there and that even the dangerous stuff, like jumping from the garage roof or playing chicken, was magical.

Maybe that notion was fueled by my and Wes's obsession with all things martial arts. We'd been watching a lot of Steven Segal movies and instead of Mom enrolling us both in karate, Dad bought us Chinese throwing stars. He wouldn't let us get a trampoline, saying, "I don't have you in braces so that you can knock out your teeth," but somehow, weapons made the cut. He went to the hardware store and bought a wooden board and drew the outline of a person on it for us to throw at. He even drew a face. Smiling. Dad had enough confidence in our sibling love and rivalry to leave us without a set of rules or instructions. He always said, "Brothers aren't for friendship, they're for justice."

That summer, my brother Wes and I could still settle everything by "killing Mr. Wood." If one of us had to stay home to babysit our little sister, Dooly, we took it to the alley. Who got the last porkchop? Kill Mr. Wood and it was yours. If we could've settled jealousy, we would've thrown for that, too. We determined that any blow to the heart, neck, or the top of the head was a kill—not to the face, that was Wes's rule. He argued that the average person wouldn't die by a thrown star to the face. Eventually we began signing and dating our kills until Mr. Wood looked, from a distance, as if he were swarmed with flies.

I met Sal while my brother and I were throwing stars in the alley. He walked up behind us and startled Wes so badly that he released his star a moment too late and it struck the garage door instead.

"You missed, fucker," I grimaced. Wes would have to mow the lawn.

"Can I try?" Sal asked from behind.

I turned to the new kid thinking we could use a little fresh blood on our kickball team and said, "You can throw Lawn Mower Man's star."

Sal lived in the split family on the other side of the radiators. He was a beanpole of a kid who cinched his belt so tight around his hipless waist that his pants doubled over in the back. His face was smooth and flawless, like puberty couldn't touch him even though he was almost sixteen. At school, he hung out with farm girls (the ones who rode the bus to school after a full morning of milking or feeding or collecting eggs) while my friends were the kids of people like my parents who lived in fancy houses and had central air conditioning and mud rooms. Sal had a sister and a mom but no dad to speak of, so I guess it was no surprise he liked hanging out with girls.

Sal pulled Wes's star out of Mr. Wood and, motioning to our rental, asked, "You live here?"

"We do for now, anyway. It's a piece of shit, but I got the nice room with the sweet sundeck."

Sal fingered the sharp points of the throwing star. "I live in that house," he jerked his head toward the humble duplex. "Trade you rooms if I hit the head."

Wes and I didn't play like that. It was kill or no kill and if there was a debate, we'd call Dad in to verify the location of major arteries.

"You ever thrown one of these before?" I asked.

"Never."

I didn't bother explaining the technical rules. "It's a deal, then. Good fuckin' luck, dude." We shook hands.

Some lucky shot. He hit Mr. Wood right in the eye, which is technically the head even though by Wes and my rules, it wasn't a kill. We argued about it for awhile until he said, "If you're gonna be a cheat, keep your stupid room with the *sweet sundeck*, you spoiled pussy."

"I'm not spoiled," I said.

"If you say so," he said. "Wanna come over?" And just like that, we were friends.

BEN IS HOLDING A PLASTIC DRAGON figure his sister Marla gave him this morning. When he was younger, Shelly and I used to let him wear a cape wherever he wanted. The day he turned eight, he came to me wearing it and asked if I'd come with him to the roof. When we got there, he untied the string from his neck, balled the cape up in his small fist and threw it over the edge of our apartment and into the alley dumpster below. We both watched it fall, billowing up like some misplaced jellyfish, and then I turned to see his face. That's when he said, "It's okay, Dad," and we went inside.

"Do you know the names of the moms and dads I'm going to see at your party?" I ask.

"Oh, god. Are you guys going to embarrass me?"

"No. I mean, I'll try not to. I think I'm pretty good at paint ball, right?"

"You're decent."

"Look, parents are there to be sure no one gets hurt, to gather up the gifts and the cards. To cut the cake. Then, we drive you home."

"I don't know why you and Mom both have to be there."

"Ben. It's your birthday. You're our son. That's what people do."

"Well, they don't have to. I mean, not everyone does that. Aaron's dad won't be there." That's because Aaron's dad is sleeping with a woman who is not Aaron's mom. Ben knows they're separated but he's using it against me anyway. And then he continues, "And I don't know why Marla has to be there."

I wonder if he'd feel differently if he had a brother rather than a sister. Wes was good for the spirit in the way that mild bullying is good for a kid with an inflated ego. But Ben doesn't talk to Marla and he doesn't talk to me. I am grateful for Bret all of a sudden. I hope they can create a brotherhood of boys who aren't afraid to talk, to ask questions, to tell one another what scares them.

THE SUMMER I MET SAL, my mother grew protective in a way I had not witnessed before. She allowed my brother and I to fight it out, to throw at Mr. Wood. But with Sal, she used rescue instincts—food, water, a comforting place to stay. And he always found his way back to our den, lured by taco night and the seeming democracy of a two-parent household.

I only ever ate lunch at Sal's. Which is to say that his mom, too tired from waiting tables, placed boxes and jars of snack food on the kitchen table (Cheez-its, Slim Jims, pickles, Tasty Kakes) and we grazed while she napped on the couch or watched *Sally Jesse*. Sal's older sister, who was curvy and pouted most of the time, occasionally joined us in card-tossing if she was bored enough and wasn't putting on mascara or whispering on the phone with her boyfriend. If the weather was crappy, we could waste a whole summer day perfecting the wrist flick that could land a card in an open hat eight feet away. If the weather was nice, we took our skateboards to the alley or our dirt bikes to the acreage out west of town that my dad owned.

Wes and I used to go together to the acreage, but he didn't want to go anymore once he found a girlfriend. And since I had a friend like Sal who took away any pangs I had for a girl of my own, and he had a sister who had black, shiny hair she tossed around for my benefit, I didn't need Wes anymore. Sal and I would set up jumps and obstacles in the field and get farmer's sunburns and then ride home near dark when Mom would feed us. From time to time, Chew would ride over on the tractor to see what we were up to. Sometimes, he'd offer us cold drinks or the use of his toilet.

Chew and Paula Turner lived in the modest farmhouse on the property with a couple of unfriendly dogs and cats that multiplied. Not long after I first took Sal to the acreage, Chew hired him to work odd jobs for extra cash. He seemed to always have work: a barn to paint, chickens to feed, equipment to wash. And since he spent so much time working for Chew, sometimes late into the evening when he returned to our house looking sad and old, he didn't want to ride out to the fields as much, so we spent more time skating in the alley or throwing stars.

"You should be grateful we kept this from Gramma." I say to Ben.

"I should?"

Now I'm holding something over his head. Shelly would call it *stealing his power*. It's not that. He really should be thankful Shelly's mom won't be there to make him go through the humiliation of the birthday paddle where he crawls through the legs of thirteen people as they smack him on the ass. We've spared him that, at least until Tuesday when everyone comes for his family birthday dinner.

"So who's going to be there? Aaron... and Bret, of course. Who else?"

"Why *of course*?" Ben says.

"Because he's your best friend."

"Oh. Well, I have a lot of *other* friends."

"Yeah, okay. But he's your special friend," I say.

Ben widens his eyes at me. "Dad, that's so queer."

"Don't use that word," I say. We have drawn lines in the sand about language.

"Oh, God. You sound like Mom." He knows I rarely enforce her rules. It's one of the ways we operate our own, exclusive universe and his disapproval further jeopardizes my membership. Before Ben started rejecting our outings, we would get buzzed on energy drinks and burp, and never tell Shelly about where we'd been or what we'd done.

"You don't mean *queer* so don't use it," I say. The word has the effect of a bass drum rattling my molars.

"Then don't call Bret my *special friend*. It's so, like, *Sesame Street*."

MID-SUMMER, I SPENT a whole day combing through Wes's and my cassette collection handpicking songs for a mixtape for Sal. He was turning sixteen in a week, and I'd already gotten him new two-tone wheels for his skateboard, but a few tracks from Van Halen's 1984 album were a celebration all their own. I was using my best handwriting to copy the playlist on the inside of the tape case when Wes barged into my room.

"You been using my tapes, you little shit?"

"They're both of ours, Wes."

"Yeah, well you could've asked permission," he said, snatching the case from my desk. "Oh, isn't that cute. You made a little mixtape for your boyfriend."

"You're such a dick," I said.

He inspected the case. "Dude, there's like, ballads on this."

"They're good songs."

"They're songs you make out to. Like, with a girl. You don't put them on your friend's mixtape. Woah. Wait."

And then his face changed, because of the fleeting possibility that I had betrayed the fellowship of rough boys. He, who had not so long before wrestled with me on gravel, put his head in my groin and said, *You're such a queer* when I told him, in a rash but tender moment, that I had only kissed two girls. Now, he backed away from me, his eyes spinning like records, and I waited for his face to change, for him to become Wes again. In that moment, he might've been questioning whether words make the man, whether this was his punishment for the hazing. Then he lunged at my throat with both hands and threw me on the bed. He was squeezing so hard that I couldn't even gasp, my vision was spotty, his shaggy hair was obscuring his face as he pressed down. It was the onset of darkness that terrified me. My head pulsed. I did not want to see hate on his face, so I closed my eyes. That's when he released his hands and spit the word *faggot* in my face before he got up and slammed the door.

"ARE THERE GOING TO BE ANY GIRLS there today?" I ask Ben, hoping he'll lighten up.

"Yeah. Mom, Marla, Mrs. Trask..."

"What about the Singleton girl you worked on the science fair project with earlier this year?"

"Jamie?"

"Yeah, her."

"She won't be there, Dad. This is a paintball party. Guys are coming in camo, I think."

"So?"

"So, we're not dancing or like going to the mall or anything. We're shooting each other with paint."

Ben flips down the visor and inspects himself in the mirror. He could use a haircut, but he refuses. My guess is he wants to look more like Bret. He takes off his glasses and rubs away the dimples the nose pads have made there.

"See, don't you think I look better without glasses?" he asks. Shelly has said no to contacts until he's sixteen, when he's more responsible and won't lose them or keep them in so long they adhere to his eyeballs.

"I wouldn't be able to see you at all if I didn't have mine."

"Dad," he demands, like he's disappointed by my joke.

"I think you're a good looking kid no matter what you do. Hair long or short, glasses or not." He rolls his eyes and we grow quiet again.

BY THE TIME IT WAS SAL'S BIRTHDAY, Mom and Dad had noticed that Wes and I had stopped talking. Mom insisted on throwing Sal a family party and baking him a lopsided cake in her lopsided oven and everyone, except for Wes, sang and clapped as he blew out sixteen candles.

Wes had to make a big scene at the dinner table. "Why don't you give Sal his queer gift now, huh Grant?"

"It's not queer, *you're* queer," I said, furious.

"Boys!" Mom said, more for Sal and Marla's sake than anyone else's. "We're trying to have a nice evening. If you wouldn't mind leaving your squabble aside, I'm sure Sal would appreciate it."

"It's okay, Mrs. Masterson," Sal said. And then, "Can I have another slice of cake, please?" like he couldn't be touched. Like he existed in a realm where wounds weren't possible, and I wished I existed there, too.

Wes and I were grounded for the weekend for *being rude in the presence of company.*

I whined, "It's not company, Mom. It's Sal," to which Wes retorted, "Yeah, Mom, when Grant and Sal get married, he'll be family, so it's not like..."

Mom drew a finger, which she never did, because pointing was also rude in her book, and said, "Mr. Wesley Masterson, I've had enough. Just because you've got a girlfriend doesn't give you license to taunt and gloat. Sal is a guest. Show some respect."

I did give the mixtape to Sal, but not on his birthday because Wes had effectively perverted the moment. I do know it was the tape that spent the most time in his Walkman that summer. A few days later, when I was finished being grounded, I set up a new trick course in the alley for Sal and I to skate through. He told me about a party at the Hardwick farm, like he'd only go if I wanted to.

"Yeah, I want to go. How'd you find out?"

"Heather Hardwick asks me every year. Just a bunch of drunk kids making out in barns. But, if you want to ride out, we can go."

Later that night, he showed up in the alley on his bike with a flashlight duct-taped between his handlebars. I had been working on growing a few facial hairs that I allowed to coil up at the base of my chin, the way a balding man salvages the remaining strands on his head. But for this party I'd shaved, I'd showered, I'd tucked my throwing star into its pouch and then into my pocket in case I'd need to impress someone or defend myself. Country roads were scarier than alleyways, infrequently traveled so that bad things had fewer eyes to witness them.

"Look who thinks he's gonna get laid," Sal said as I opened the gate into the alley. It had taken me three changes to decide on jeans, my Phillies tee, and new checkered Vans.

"We've gotta try, right?" I said. "Besides, farm girls are easy."

"They are?" Sal said. "I just thought that they're friendly."

"I dunno."

"Oh."

Sal and I rode in tandem out to the farm, past my father's acreage, on back roads and through freshly cut fields. We didn't talk, the wind was too loud in our ears, but we played follow the leader the whole way, which wasn't fair for Sal because he couldn't do a good wheelie. As soon as we crested Fox Ridge, we could see the glow of taillights and a small fire. The last daylight had been wrung from the horizon so we let ourselves be guided by the distant flickerings ahead.

The Hardwicks raised veal calves. In the darkness, the pens looked like small mausoleums and the calves like zombies hanging their heads through the arched openings. Heather Hardwick staggered out from behind them, buttoning her pants and I let out a high-pitched yelp. She was laughing, probably at me, or maybe at our dirt bikes, but she said, "You made it!" throwing her arms around Sal and nearly knocking him off his bike. He held his head away from her, which seemed to draw her closer to him. I took note of his nonchalance, and tried it on for the evening, hoping it might earn me the same attention.

BEN AND I HAVE GONE TO CAMDEN SUPERFUN a couple times a year since he was ten. Last month, when we'd planned to go, he cancelled on me saying he didn't feel well but spent the whole day in his room watching YouTube while I did yard work.

"We haven't been to Superfun in a while," I finally say.

"I have. You haven't." Ben scratches away the paint on the wing of his toy dragon.

"Oh. I didn't realize you still go."

"You don't realize a lot of things."

I think about how I listen at his door but can't turn the doorknob, how we throw the baseball in the backyard, the snap of the ball in leather the only sound between us. I think about the times I've been cold or instructive or distant. I think about that day: the bike in Chew's pick-up, no flat-tire, perfect for riding, the wheels so still even as I checked over my shoulder when I rode away. So I say, "Ben. Tell me then. What don't I realize?"

As I hope for his answer to break the long quiet, I think about how different the night at the farm might've been if we really would've gotten laid, if that was something each of us even wanted. Earlier that year, I had hung my arm around Marcie Green's shoulders and, like a crane, slowly lowered my hand into her loosely fitting blouse while we watched some lame arm-wrestling movie with Sylvester Stallone in her basement. I had tried to find a nipple and she kind of bit her lip while I did and that was that.

AT THE FARM, IF IT COULD'VE BEEN that easy, Sal and I could've wandered away from the small bonfire and the cases of Keystone beer, our arms around fresh girls, to a place in the barn where only faint laughter and distant radio waves could be heard spreading out like a thin layer over the night-time farmland, no interference as the silos connected every farm in the valley. Beneath them we could have groped and grunted and panted and fumbled and been scared of our own potential, while the radio waves floated easily above us, making music of it all.

But Sal and I didn't wander away with fresh girls, and he didn't introduce me to anyone. He didn't say to Heather Hardwick, "You remember Grant," which most likely she didn't, but still. I would've even settled for: "This is Grant. He wants to see if your boobs feel like dough." This would've given me an in—an embarrassing in, but an in nonetheless. Kids at school had trademarks that made them memorable, but I was just plain Grant. I trailed behind Heather and Sal like a hungry puppy until they reached the bonfire, and someone handed me a bottle of Jack Daniels. There must've been fifty kids, mostly farm kids and Vo-Tech kids who went to school half time and trade school the other half to be welders or cooks or beauticians. I recognized Cheap Charlie Willis and Mike the Beaver right away because they were inseparable and dressed alike in concert tees and torn jeans. I had made an extra effort to dress like I didn't care, too.

I stood watching people move in constellations of threes toward the beer, away from the fire, into the corn, under the darkness. Girls giggled and tipped their heads back while boys watched for the flash of white beneath their necks where they might be lucky enough to press their lips. Pretty Jenny Skelling jumped off a flat bed and came over to wish Sal a happy birthday. Then she turned to me, trying to engage me to gain ground with Sal and said, "You're Wes's brother, right?"

"Yeah. Grant." I extended my hand, but she planted a kiss on my cheek instead, watching Sal out of the corner of her eye. The farm girls he hung out with were deliciously soft, smelled like fresh milk, had creamy complexions, and long, shiny hair. Each one of them looked at him longingly and because I knew he didn't want any of them, I felt even more privileged to be his friend. That had something to do with why my other friends fell away that summer, mystified by my absence, my seldom appearance at their parties which were held in game-rooms or poolside with wine coolers and access to the old man's liquor cabinet.

Sal wandered away with the girls and I sat down on a log by the fire drinking from each passed bottle until I couldn't distinguish faces from flames. We had ridden our bikes across Dad's acreage to get to the farm and when I looked back in that direction, the fields were pulsing with fireflies like tiny, inconstant beacons.

BEN TURNS TO ME, SHOWS ME the full measure of his curious face, and says, "Grown-ups worry about how their kid's gonna turn out, huh? You ask all these hard questions and then talk about them with other adults to decode the answers. But who asks grown-ups questions like that?"

"I dunno. I guess we ask each other," I say. He takes few risks like this because silence has a way of swallowing everything up. I struggle to hide that I am nervous and weak. "You wanna ask me a question?"

He says, "I want to know why that article Gramma sent you makes you so sad."

"It doesn't make me sad. It makes me think." I am trying to be honest, but the pursuit terrifies me.

"It makes you think so much you can't sleep?"

Now I know he's seen me, these last few nights, reading and rereading the article and hunched over a box of old photographs, a heavy glass nearby and the unhealthy euphoria of insomnia letting the memory in. I found only a handful of pictures from the summer I met Sal. He is in only two of them. One, which Mom took, is a brown wash of candle glow with Sal's waxy face puffing, illuminated like a jack-o-lantern over the birthday cake. The other features Sal and I with our skateboards, standing in the alley, a trick course set up in the background, our hair messy and damp with sweat. I can remember that day, one of mutual adoration as we set and accomplished new tricks, kept score, were big shots. That's what my face reveals—the way I'm smirking at the lens. But Sal's eyes are far away, stuck on something distant and secret. That's the part I spent last night trying to unearth.

I realize Ben's waiting for my answer with a patience unknown to thirteen-year-olds.

"Yeah. I guess that's why I can't sleep," I say.

"Did you know that man?" he asks.

"Mr. Turner? I did know him, yes." My mouth twitches at the corners as I await his next question. Most likely, he wants to know why I've been up late, sleepless, and what that man did to make him bad.

He knows enough to just say, "Oh."

A FEW HOURS LATER, WHEN SAL returned from winning girls' hearts and the admiration of awkward boys, he was sweaty and slack-jawed.

"You cool?" he asked.

"I'm drunk."

"Me too," he said, helping me up from my place on the log. "You have a good time?"

"I guess. I feel like shit, though. I can't go home like this."

"No one says we have to." At the time, it seemed that Sal did not live in fear, nor was he guided by household or personal rules, and even when his plans were devious, they were not complicated by morality. "We can sleep in the barn for a few hours and ride home before your mom wakes up."

I thought that's what we both did, but when I awoke to the first deep blue slits of morning creeping through the barn walls, he was gone. Outside, the embers in the fire pit cooled and a few remaining cars with fogged windows and snoozing bodies remained like large stones against the mild hunches of mountains. Sal's bike was gone too, and with the sun nearly ready to break, I didn't have much of a choice but to leave without him.

I decided to ride the way we'd come, in case something had happened to him. I felt for the throwing star in my pocket and mounted my bike. I don't know how I managed to ride straight, let alone back through the rough-cut fields, towards my father's acreage. I would have killed for a glass of water and remembered the brook that ran along the west side of Chew's farmhouse. I stopped to contemplate its cleanliness and that's when I saw it. In the steady blue of pre-dawn, Sal's dirt bike in the back of Chew's pick-up, leaned against the wheel well, having been ridden here or loaded into the truck at the Hardwick's farm, placed there by the boy or the farmer, with the promise of a ride home or a cold drink or a warm place to sleep? I could not know. I rode away.

BEN AND I ARE SEALED IN THE CAR, thirteen balloons filling the back seat, the rain incessantly tapping its fingers on the windows, the radio off, the air still.

I say, "I'd like to tell you about my friend Sal some time." I will spare him my uncertainty, my fears, I will not describe the misplaced feeling of betrayal that turned us away from one another that summer. But I will tell him about how I learned to throw cards and stars and talked more than I ever have, sometimes until I fell asleep. That is how I will do it.

Ben allows me my chance and says, "You wanna tell me now?"

"Not right now. But some time soon."

I DIDN'T SEE SAL FOR ALMOST A WEEK after the party. I was angry at him for leaving me to get drunk by the fire, and then in the barn, angry at my own insignificance, angry that Wes had a girlfriend and that no one ever remembered me. Sal was supposed to remember me. But he had left me and now he hadn't come around for days and because I was confused, I was too paralyzed to knock on his door.

I was throwing stars at Mr. Wood when Sal came riding around the corner so fast I thought he was running from something. He burned his back wheel on the gravel and stopped suddenly, as if from fear or guilt, and swept the hair from his face before stepping off his bike.

"Where you been?" he said.

"Me? I've been here. What about you?"

Now that I'm no longer a boy, but a father to one, I know how they operate. Emotions are more aptly drawn out by mothers or girlfriends. Or, by throwing punches.

"You pussy. Why don't you just ask me?" Sal said, shoving me.

"Ask you what?"

"You know what," he said, shoving me harder. I didn't know what he meant, though. I just felt the same way I'd been feeling my whole life—belittled by Wes's shadow, like

I'd been duped again by someone cooler, more experienced, more desirable.

"Okay. Why'd you leave me?" I asked, kicking the gravel with the toe of my shoe.

"Oh, sure. Get at the real question by asking another one."

"Sal, you left me sleeping in the barn. I didn't know where you'd gone, if something had happened to you... you just disappeared. What am I supposed to think?"

"Think what your brother thinks," he commanded, because maybe he thought it would be easier to concede to Wes's mistruths than for Sal to tell me things I wasn't prepared to know.

"My brother's not right," I said. But as the words came out, I didn't know what I believed, just that I felt betrayed by something—not Sal, not Wes, not even Chew Turner who, I realize now, was guilty as hell. I cannot name, now, what it was then. Maybe I was betrayed by my own insecurity, that I was not brave enough to overcome my confusion.

AT THE END OF THAT SUMMER, we moved overseas as we'd planned four months prior. When I returned two years later, everyone had graduated, including Sal. I kept up with the boys like me who didn't have names to remember them by. During college breaks and some summers before our grades earned us work opportunities in Washington and Manhattan, we shook hands with each other's parents and took our shoes off in mud rooms and brought small gifts to family cocktail parties. I asked my mother about Sal, since she was a woman who, by her own account, was not part of the perpetual loop of town gossip, but rather a stone in the stream over which information flowed. She had nothing to report, although she said, *I do wonder about that sweet, misguided boy.* One winter break I thought I saw him ducking into a beat-up Honda with an "OHO Pizza" sign illuminated on the top. It was a man of his build, anyway, but the face was too much a blur in the snowfall for me to be sure.

WHEN WE PULL INTO THE LOT AT Camden's Superfun, there are already a few kids huddled under the front awning waiting for the birthday boy. He kind of smirks until he sees Bret, the friend he seeks to impress, and then his mouth explodes into a full-faced snaggle-toothed smile. Boys go through a kind of same-sex courtship sometime around Ben's age, when dads lose their luster. They like each other's stuff (their cool shoes, their new gadgets), but they're mostly interested in what they can *do*. Sal was able to kill Mr. Wood in one try.

I drop Ben off and as I pull away, he high-fives Bret before they disappear through the door. When I go inside, my wife will hand me a protective vest, tell me I'm on Ben's team, which is almost worse than being the enemy. I'll have to protect him. I'll try to be as good as Bret but not better than him. I'll dive and barrel roll and army crawl just a foot behind Ben and he will shake me off, scornfully, saying, "Stop following me, Dad." Bret will be the one to stop what he's doing and look at me, his mouth in an "o" of wonder. I will think of Sal again, he will keep me up tonight too, I will wonder if things might've been different if I'd known what to ask him that day, if I wasn't so afraid of what he might've been telling me.

I will always wonder what it would have taken to protect him. When I look at the photograph of us in the alley, I must guess that what his eyes were making out in the distance was the image of himself as he wanted to be—the image, he knew, only I saw. I will try to tell Ben about Sal some time, but my uncertainty will creep in and make a mess of the memory. I will look as if I've lost track of things, my mind groping for the unseen, distance-dimmed stars of the memory of that summer. Ben's face will take to pity, and all I will be able to muster will be, "Keep talking, Ben. Don't go quiet on me."

The Fells

In college, Lena's boyfriend showed her his cat cadaver, an orange tabby he called Ms. Woo, who died in childbirth, two of the kittens remaining in utero. In the lab, Lena dared to stroke the matted fur of the cat's belly but hadn't closed her eyes fast enough to avoid the skin, peeled-back like cold rubber, revealing two faces still pink and hairless.

Some days the baby inside her was a rabbit, a gopher, a pack of dead kittens and other times it was a fruit, or the fruit bowl itself. *The size of a cantaloupe* is what Dr. Simon said, so that's what she pictured there: a pickled melon, floating in a jar, its flesh muted and waterlogged. For Lena, the baby was coming, and it couldn't be stopped without unraveling her.

She had slept, the last few months, with her back towards Michael, awake with dread. The year before, at a routine check-up, her gynecologist had told her to let her know when she and Michael were considering having children. *Because then*, the doctor said, *we can address your inability to ovulate.* This news had come with a kind of private elation. It removed from her the pressures of conceiving, the determined nature of "trying." It eclipsed the deep-down incongruity she felt about not wanting a baby. Now Lena lay awake, pregnant and barely breathing, thinking that if she were still enough, and the baby were too, it might not exist at all.

THE LEAVES WERE ORANGE in the new chill of late October so that when Lena's Subaru crested the hill and turned into the parking lot of Fells Woods Recreation area, she felt the seasonal change in the light on her skin, coming down through the lattice leaves above her. She pulled into a parking spot and cut the engine. She was grateful that she didn't recognize anyone standing in the field. She had only come to walk, to sit and watch her dog, Ernie, fetch and swim. She clung to the simplicity of these outings because, soon enough, they would be different, though she avoided speculating *how*. On her walks, when she encountered people who remembered her name, whose dogs sniffed at her belly and scratched their paws in the dirt, protecting her, she felt the responsibility of conversation—the sense that the world itself was filled with people who did not shrug one another off.

She ducked under a branch and onto the widened path, where the ferns shriveled, their little fingers yellowing at the onset of cool weather. Ernie raced ahead of her, his shaggy brown tail wagging in the air. He bolted left when he caught scent of the water while the rhythm of Lena's feet kept pace with her thoughts.

The days were getting shorter, and she only had an hour before the trails would grow shadowy and cold. Last summer, when the days were longer and Michael's company let employees out early on Fridays, they sometimes walked across the Massachusetts Avenue bridge, into the city to drink fifteen-dollar cocktails. On the way home, half-drunk, wind whipping in all directions, they would stop at the exact midpoint, halfway between Cambridge and Boston and look down river and throw pennies for luck or wishes. Michael would yell his wish in the wind while she protested, *You can't tell me, it won't come true!* He always replied, *You know them already!* And she did. He kept nothing secret. He was an eternal optimist with boyish tendencies to fawn over her and tell her she was beautiful or that she smelled good when she'd been digging in the garden. He had leaned around her once when she was dropping her penny in the Charles and said, *I wish that you never have to wish.*

Ernie, ahead in the distance, scampered up a rock bank and surveyed the terrain. He was waiting for Lena, checking on her, and seeing that she was close behind, he started off again, confident in their partnership.

This morning when Michael dropped her at the hospital's main entrance, Lena loitered in the lobby even though she was late for the appointment. She was performing a silent experiment to see how many people glanced at her belly which looked more like a basketball beneath her shirt than a baby. If she were treated preferentially—if doors were held or places in line given over, she would knit her eyebrows, deny their kindnesses. In the lobby cafe, she poured a large cup of coffee. The cashier smiled and said, *boy or girl?* and, without answering, she walked to the elevators and pressed the button. That's when she remembered a snapshot of last night's dream: her mother's freshly painted mouth hysterical in laughter as she jostled the newborn in her arms until it turned slowly to Jell-O and fell away from her grasp in pieces.

The elevator opened to the sixth floor. The waiting room was half filled with silently speculative women and their partners. A thin-lipped woman in her forties nervously organized her handbag. Another woman, the mask of melasma on her face, closed her eyes and leaned against her husband. No one appeared joyful or expectant. No one talked. Maybe they were feeling what she felt. Terror. Regret. Inadequacy. Maybe this is what waiting looked like. Lena grew conscious of her staring. She felt ashamed for resenting the baby that grew inside her in the face of the doctor's diagnosis. Michael liked to use their circumstances when she sobbed and swore and was blue all day. He'd say *this is our own kind of miracle, Lena,* his eyes groping her face for any last shred of faith.

Michael arrived and flounced into the seat beside her, bringing in with him the smell of the lobby: the bakery's croissants and antiseptic cleaner.

"You check in?" he said, too loudly.

She shook her head. She'd forgotten—too overwhelmed by the scene. He approached the desk and returned (*all set*) and plucked the sports section from a nearby table. Lena closed her eyes and bowed her head and imagined every woman in that room, their babies now floating in bubbles above their heads, drifting toward the skylight, bumping it so gently, making the sound of balloons on glass, floating up, up, up and into the atmosphere. There they would be safe, out of harm's hands, distant from cruelty, from her own worried mind, her indecision, her impatience, her sadness. There the babies would be safe to inherit nothing.

The ultrasound showed the amphibious sack, a hydrocephalic newt of a thing with shadows for organs. The heart was pixil and beat, pattering on, pattering on, a gray sputtering smudge. And though she hadn't been asked if she'd wanted to see the baby in three dimensions, that's what she got—every distortion and amplification creating a more terrifying image for Lena. The baby's lidded eyes were sunken, its lips inflated and puckered, fluid membranes streaked across its face like milfoil in the bottom of a great lake. *Do you know the sex of your baby?* the technician had asked. *No, no thank you*, Lena replied as if refusing its existence all together. That's when Lena saw Michael frown, just the slightest downward turn of his lips. The woman printed two eight-and-a-half by eleven slides, one in pink, another in blue, saying, *for the fridge*, and handed them to Michael. *The doctor will be right in.*

In the car on the way home, Michael tried to make her laugh, puckering his lips—open, close, open, close.

"Stop it," she said tersely.

"C'mon, Lena. Those lips are mine, you know." He moved a hand to her thigh for a squeeze. "Boy or girl?" he said.

"Or prehistoric creature of the deep?"

"Jesus, Lena."

"I'm sorry."

"Why are you so fucking miserable?"

She couldn't explain. "I'm incapable," she finally said.

"No you're not. You say that like a person who doesn't have a choice."

"I *don't* have a choice, Michael," she said, taking hold of the dashboard.

"You do! You have the power and the choice to accept this knowing it's not ideal, or you can wallow and be miserable and let it eat you alive."

"This is not what I wanted."

"But this is what happened," he said. Lena buried her face in her hands and began to cry. Almost in her third trimester and her heart had not changed. "Did you *never* want this for us?"

She felt sick in the recycled air of the car. "I wanted to know first that I *wanted* a baby and *then* get pregnant."

"Jesus, Lena. You can't make *all* the choices!"

"But Michael, in my whole life, I've never felt that thing that some women get. That thing that says *I just can't wait to be a mother*. It's not part of my understanding of the world." Michael cracked a window, his own unanticipated sickness creeping in his throat, and inventoried their slim history of family planning discussions. Child-bearing had not factored heavily in their momentum to get married. "What if the fact that that instinct has never surfaced in me is a sign that I'm not supposed to be a mother?"

"You'll read *that* sign but you'll refuse to admit that this is a god damned *miracle*, Lena? Nobody, including the doctor, even thought this was a possibility."

"You think I'm being selfish?"

"I think you're not allowing yourself any mistakes."

"But what if *this* is a mistake? What if we should've…"

"Married people don't have abortions, Lena."

"Most married people have decided they *want* children, I think." She hesitated. "What if I don't want it? What if I can't love it? Or if I'd rather leave it gasping for air in its crib, or out in the cold because it's too terrifying to live with? These are real thoughts I have, Michael."

"I didn't marry a monster, Lena."

"But, what if none of this changes? I'm not like you. I'm ungrateful, I'm cruel."

"You're not."

"I am. You've thought it. And at some point in all of this, you'll tell me. It will come to that."

"Why are you so dark? You've got a tiny baby in there, a baby we've seen, heart-beating and kicking and everything."

"And I can only think about how things will never be the way they were."

"What if they're better?"

"What if I don't want to find that out?"

She'd let him too far in. She protected her mood from him most of the time, going for long walks, sometimes without water and enough sustenance in her system so that she felt light-headed and ethereal and high. Sometimes she imagined that she was starving the baby, depleting every cell until it shrunk back inside her the way she envisioned it formed, like a pearl inside an oyster in reverse, until the baby was absorbed into the pink flesh of her insides. And when she could not imagine the baby away, she imagined herself along a typically traveled hiking trail like the one she walked now, leaving the baby tucked into a basket beneath layers of clean linen to be found by delighted picnickers.

The dog swam in the water making figure eights with his barrel-like body. He was looking at her expectantly, waiting for her verdict: pride or disappointment? He climbed out and onto the rock bank and shook his thick, brown coat.

"Hey, you," a man's voice called.

Lena startled. She recognized the dog approaching her, its owner trailing behind. "Oh, hey." It was Bruce, or Chuck, or another monosyllabic name. He was broad-chested, his head topped with a thinning cap of peach-colored hair. He drove a maroon van that reminded her of the kind her mother told her to avoid as a child. Lena remembered talking with him briefly on several occasions, his foul mouth making an impression on her.

"Who's this again?" he asked, gesturing to her dog.

"This is Ernie. And who's that?" Lena asked, referring to the dog who sniffed gingerly at Ernie's neck and face, his nose twitching in approval.

"This is Zappa. But I've got three. The other ones are up at my girlfriend's place." He cocked his head on his thick neck and said, "Zaps, you miss Diva and Chucky don't you?" Zappa snapped his jaws together in response. "You're the loyal one, Zaps, aren't you boy?" People who spoke to their pets had a way of endearing themselves to her.

Lena stood watching the dogs wag and inspect one another, hoping that if she said nothing he'd walk on, that she could return to her private revelry. But, he remained like a great oak rooted to the earth. "I've seen you here before, haven't I?"

"Yeah. We come a few times a week." The dogs had stopped their inventory and now Lena stared at Zappa's one glacier blue eye which seemed to be tracking her.

"It's a boy, you know," the man said.

"Zappa. Yeah, I figured. Like Frank Zappa."

"No. The baby," he said, gesturing to Lena's stomach.

"Oh, *that*."

"I can see it in your face."

"Oh." She wondered if it was the fullness of her face, the dark circles beneath her eyes, her hair darkening, but she didn't care to ask, the way she didn't care to discover the sex of the thing.

She beckoned Ernie with a whistle, walked on, hoping this man might choose a different path.

"I've got two sons, so I know. Chad and Brian."

"Oh. Well, congrats, then." She said dismissively, over her shoulder.

"They're grown."

"Still."

"Still what? I didn't do nothin'. My wife raised 'em mostly, and one's a twat just like her." She hadn't heard that word in a decade. Her heart quickened. "I'm sorry," he said. "He's an *asshole* just like his mother."

She had a special gift for imagining alternate circumstances and summoning them for comfort. If her belly were a balloon, she could float right up into the tree canopy so she wouldn't have to apologize as she excused herself, so she wouldn't have to break into a trot at twenty seven weeks. She wouldn't have to be caught looking nervous. She'd just float up, up, up and the trees would draw back their needles so she'd be safe, eventually drifting through the clouds and then into the atmosphere.

Agency in her life seemed to have dissolved months ago. Would challenging her intuition change it? What if this man, with his home-dyed hair and his vulgarity, had something to offer, however unexpected, about the state of parenthood? What if she engaged him in conversation, if she put her faith in good-will rather than heeding the slow terror overcoming her?

"How'd you find it? Being a parent, I mean." She asked.

"How did I *find* it?" He repeated. "I found it with my dick, and nine months later the bitch had a baby."

She swallowed hard. What if her engagement in the conversation became solicitation? What if his words were threats? He repulsed her. Her alternative scenarios turned darker: him pushing her up against a tree and assaulting her, him beating her with a rock and running off with the dogs.

"Which way you going?" he asked. They were nearly at the farthest point on the path from the parking lot where the trails forked. One trail squared away from the reservoir, headed over a small ridge, and dumped into the lot. The other, the longer route, hugged the reservoir. She knew that voices traveled across water, and she wanted to remain in its view, just in case.

She shrugged. She didn't know what words to summon to make him leave her in peace. *I want to be alone*, or, *Please stop following me.* They wouldn't come. If she angered him, what would he do? If she could commit to being casual would it make him less threatening? "Doesn't matter. You?" she finally said.

"I'm following you. Feel like company."

It was possible she was paranoid. Her brain was fatigued. Her body was on guard. The dogs ran up ahead, weaving in and out of trees, making a game of chasing and tumbling, the nature of their companionship distilled to a series of muscles twitching and rippling beneath their shiny coats, their instincts otherworldly. To Ernie, this Zappa had been vetted. He smelled safe. Ernie would be of no help now if this man were to attack her. He would instead perceive this man as friend and travel farther and farther out onto the rocky banks before he returned at her calling. And because it seemed this man was wild and blunt, consciously rude, aware of his bad habits enough to amend them, because maybe somehow she was the brute, reluctant love still failing to soften her, she tried this: "I don't really want it."

"You were hoping for a girl, weren't you?"

"No, I wasn't hoping for anything."

Lena imagined this man sitting on a porch in Lynn with one of his sons, smoking butts to the filter, his hand on the breasts of a girl who lived in the apartment upstairs, maybe even his son's girlfriend, no one on that porch hoping for anything, everything just happening in a series of disconnected events.

"The guy's a deadbeat or something?" he said.

"No. The guy's my husband." She called after Ernie, sending a whistle searing across the surface of the reservoir.

"No shit. Well, you get along?"

"Yeah, we get along." Ernie returned and dropped a wet stick at her feet, water streaming from his underside. She tossed the stick ahead and the two dogs tore off again.

"Crazy bitches. What don't *you* want?"

"Don't call me that." She was proud to have mustered the words, though she'd doubted she'd be capable of more.

"Shit. Why are you so uptight?"

"I'm not uptight." Ernie returned with the stick, dropping it at Lena's feet again.

"Bullshit. You like to get laid?"

Solicitation, antagonization. She hadn't brought a cell phone. Never did. A leash and her keys were enough to carry and since she always chose a trusted route, she never thought she'd need one. The place was usually well populated with park rangers, other hikers, and mountain bikers. Answering either way might be an invitation. Maybe the best defense was offense.

"Do you?" she said finally, bending to pick up the stick, turning around, squaring her eyes in his, being as bold as she knew how to be. The stick in her hands might work as a weapon, but she was conscious not to hold it like one.

His lips crawled slowly away from his teeth to reveal a chipped eye tooth. She watched him take her in. The freckles on the bridge of her nose, the new sweat at her temples. The swell of her belly beneath her shirt. "That's what it was with my wife. Mind shit. That's why we can't live together anymore. I would choke her."

Her heart raced and her pupils constricted. Lena didn't break her gaze. She'd read about cell memory—the transfer of trauma from mother to fetus. What if this was precipitating trauma for a baby who grew into a fearful, anxious child. A child who never liked the woods or water.

She turned finally, quickening her pace on the trail, knowing it was another fifteen minutes back to the main lot.

"Hey, girl. You can slow down. Trail's not on fire."

"It's getting dark."

She thought of that time on the bus in Cambridge—packed with passengers, congested with the summer heat so that she couldn't tell one sensation from the next—a man pressed against her, maybe his hand or an erection in the crack of her ass so that she swatted at it with her free hand. He pressed harder into her, and her eyes widened but her voice betrayed her—no sound for anything (not surprise nor anguish nor desperation)—just the sound of what was taken away like the surprised release of the hydraulic brakes as the bus slowed to a stop.

She called after Ernie, whistling and shouting his name, but he made his way down to the water once again where a rocky ledge protruded over the edge of the reservoir. Not yet exhausted from the swimming, he defied her. "Ernie, come! No more!" she called again. She gripped the stick in her hand tighter. It had stormed earlier in the week and the water level was high, the reservoir filled with fallen branches and other floating debris. Ernie glanced at her quickly, over his shoulder, and slipped into the water. Lena moved out to the edge of the rocks where her red sneakers might make her visible to someone on the reservoir's opposite bank.

She wanted to keep the man in her periphery. Would a call for help bring his hands around her throat? Could she fight him off? Would she use the stick like a knife? Like a club? Could she push him into the reservoir and run through the woods to the parking lot?

"Zappa doesn't swim," the man said. His dog was curiously close to the edge, his back legs recoiling like springs as he watched Ernie crawl out of the water and drop a new stick at Lena's feet.

Maybe disinterest was the strategy—"Do what you want, then. Move on." Was it urgent enough? He had said *twat* and *bitch* and *crazy*. He had followed her. She tried to remind herself that she did not owe anyone anything while perhaps she thought she did. The man remained at a distance, the tips of his thick fingers shoved into the tops of his jean pockets. She could tell by the way he stood back, the insecurity of his posture, that the water was making him nervous.

"C'mon, Zapps. Time to go," he called, taking a step back, throwing his head over his shoulder, feigning departure. But the dog remained, its eyes tracking the triangle: stick, Ernie, Lena, stick, Ernie, Lena.

This was her out. She drew her arm back, the dogs' heads hypnotic, trained, and let the stick fly. Ernie shot off the rock and Zappa followed, their legs like arrows, their bodies like barrels as they hit the water. An "oh" slipped from Lena's lips—at once surprised, apologetic. She'd thought the man's dog would remain behind, aware of its limits, that it would paw at the edge of the cliff while Ernie swam, that it would bow its head in defeat and turn to go home.

"Zappa! Zapps! C'mon, pup!" He cried. Zappa twisted, his front paws thrashing while Ernie paddled out, his rear buoyant, his body blending with the dark water. "No! No! He's not a swimmer!" the man shouted, indicting her, as they both scrambled toward the rocky edge. Lena slid to a stop, her toes slipping as the rocks crumbled away and fell into the water. Zappa's head bobbed and he gasped for air. She wanted to urge him—*Jump! He needs help! Jesus, jump!* The dog's claws surfaced and thrashed, each pass pushing the tangled mass of sticks and brush in a different direction.

Lena might've heard a sound move through the man's throat—a sound like strong wind through a great tree, a sound of secret terror, and she took hold of his forearm to steady them both. It was a gesture she wouldn't remember until one day, when the baby was two and clinging to the hem of her coat, sucking on a lolly and waiting for the crosswalk to change when, suddenly, the child let go, stepped into the stream of moving traffic with a whoosh, and the woman next to her gasped and took hold of her child's wrist, squeezed it hard, all horror and hope.

The dog's eyes went cold with fear, imploring the man, its nose giving a final bobbin-tug as his body sunk down. The man jumped into the water, finally, his body going under like a boulder. Lena stopped breathing, was wordless as the man surfaced and swam like a child, his head straining toward the dog, his face wet and pale. He slapped his hands at the surface, searching the water for a sign, calling Zappa's name again and again, shrill and relentless, when finally, the dog's body rose to the surface, spine first, body limp, his head not reaching to breathe. The man swam toward him. *I'm sorry Zappa. I'm so sorry, boy.*

Ernie stood beside Lena, watching, water pooling beneath him. The stick had been retrieved and lay at Lena's feet. The man took the dog in his arms, treaded toward the edge, his face a puzzle of grief. Ernie was watching her, as she considered offering the man a hand, a way of crawling out, but she was too stunned, too wary of her guilt, a debt befallen her in minutes, the weight of it heavy as stone in the swollen well of her womb. An apology would be misplaced. She wanted to slip back onto the shadowy paths and retreat: offer privacy to this man, allow him his grief. She wouldn't forgive him for his menace, his ignorance and rough tongue, but she could offer him grace.

The man hoisted the dog's limp body onto the rocks and crawled out, one heavy boot at a time, his shirt clinging to his body, swirls of dark hair visible beneath it. He shivered, pulled Zappa onto his lap like a baby, cradled him, wept.

Back at the edge of the parking lot, Ernie hesitated, sniffed at the traces of dogs long gone, maybe of Zappa and the man, watching where the path dumped out into the field. Lena whistled for Ernie to jump in the trunk. Instead, the dog whimpered and whined and scratched in the dirt, watched the shadows grow and move at the edge of the forest. And then he laid down, a sentinel, a witness. The pink cells within Lena twitched and divided, again and again, undeterred, generous and bold. Eventually, the man would catch his breath. He would send a fat hand along the dog's belly, checking again and again for a heartbeat. When it did not come, he would carry the body home.

Up Dell Drive

When Mrs. Hamza had first taught Honey the greeting—"Salaam Alaikum"—she had thought it sounded like, "Salami, I like 'em." Now, Honey silently repeats the phrase as she watches the woman place lamb, red beans, and dates on the conveyer until she has enough courage to turn from the register and say it—"Salaam Alaikum."

"Pretty good. You've been practicing," Mrs. Hamza says, her eyes so calm and black they are unnerving.

While Mrs. Hamza digs in the great deep of the beach bag she totes in all seasons, Honey imagines this lamb, these beans, and dates in this woman's hands and tries to imagine what it will become. Mrs. Hamza, a librarian, lives alone across the street from her in a house like a brick box, its small windows kept dark by heavy velvet curtains, even in summertime. Honey remembers wondering, as a child, what the woman's feet did beneath that robe that made her appear to be floating. Once, in the library, she had trailed behind Mrs. Hamza listening closely for the soft padding of those feet thinking that everything about Mrs. Hamza was magical. Her eyes are darker than anyone's eyes Honey has ever known. She often wondered if Mrs. Hamza, and people like her, had pupils at all or if they saw with the whole, colored part of the eye. They had learned in Mrs. Kryszanski's science class how eyes worked, but still.

Mrs. Hamza finally finds her checkbook and says in a way Honey decides is neither cunning nor sympathetic, "Did your father like the books I brought him?"

"I don't know if he's read them yet, Mrs. Hamza. He's just been resting mostly."

"Please tell him that I think of him often and that I'd be happy to bring him anything he wants from the library. You may knock on my door if you think of something."

"Alright," Honey says, watching Mrs. Hamza's purple-brown lips purse as she completes the check. Suddenly, Honey cannot keep from filling up the quiet space with words. "My mom wanted me to tell you thanks for the casserole. She'll get your dish back to you soon enough."

"Oh, that was kibbeh batata. Traditional Iraqi dish," she says. Mrs. Hamza tears out the check and hands it to Honey. Her address is written in both English and the letters of Arabic that look like smoke curling in air. Honey has seen these letters in the newspapers her father keeps in the hall closet next to his uniform and the letters she wrote him while he was in Iraq. She has knelt in the bottom of that closet, imagining that it is a bunker. She has dragged her fingers along the squiggly, unfamiliar text, imagining she can read and communicate secret messages to people in languages others wouldn't understand.

"Please, take good care," says Mrs. Hamza reaching for Honey's hand the instant she withdraws it and turns toward the register. It's a gesture of kindness and Honey knows she's missed the opportunity to show Mrs. Hamza she's unafraid, unlike so many other kids in the neighborhood who claim she butchers goats in her backyard and wears the head scarf to conceal signs of torture. Honey's mother is startled every time Mrs. Hamza comes to the door, as if she's carrying bombs beneath her clothing, as if she is the reason her husband now lies in the bed upstairs, his leg blown off and his mind always tricking him.

The day before Honey's daddy was deployed, her mother threw a big barbecue for the neighbors and some of his buddies from the base who brought their girlfriends or wives and government meat for the grill and sweaty macaroni salad. Everyone wore red, white and blue and her mother ordered a big cake from the Mega-Basket that said *Rock Iraq! Good luck Sergeant Berkowski!* It was a red velvet cake, her daddy's favorite, and Honey watched him have a second piece while she pumped her legs on the makeshift patio swing they'd put up earlier that morning. The seat was wobbly—just a plank with some rope tied fast—and she was swinging like a trapeze artist, so gracefully. When she fell, she saw the ground far away and coming slowly toward her, wondering if that was what pilots saw when they got shot down. How much time do they have to know it's the end? Honey saw her daddy and he saw her, right at the same time—the exact instant she hit the patio. It was a Sunday and his breath was quick and sour with beer and he laid her across his lap while her eyes tried to focus on his face. He stroked Honey's cheek and examined her head, which felt like a big, numb rock before her eyelids closed and she drifted to sleep.

When she woke up, her head still on her daddy's lap, he was watching an old movie while the crowd outside continued their buzzing and laughing. Instead of stitches, he'd tied strands of her hair across the inch-long gash on her head (maybe he'd learned that in the service, too) and covered it with a bandage. When she reached up to feel it, he took her hand and put it against his sandpapery face instead.

Now, she reaches up and finds the scar's ridge, smooth and hard. It's time to lock her register. Mr. Huckles sits at his elevated post, behind plexiglass, like some big fish in an aquarium. He thinks it's unprofessional for employees to talk, so he's designed a series of hand gestures that employees use to signal to one another from across the store, as if the entire staff were deaf and using sign language to communicate. Honey signals the punching of a timecard and Huckles nods.

Antonio "Tuna" Maldonado is stacking cans of tomatoes in aisle four when she passes on her way to the frozen section. Honey notices his famous lips right away, slackly parted in absent-mindedness. When he spots her, he makes a "tssk" sound that she associates with movies about faraway places like Los Angeles, where teenagers speak in code. She stops. She's known Antonio since the fifth grade when his family moved from somewhere like Texas so his daddy could work at the penitentiary. Usually, penitentiary kids don't stick around more than a couple years because their dads or moms get transferred, and they're never heard from again. Tuna holds two fingers to his lips like he's smoking a joint and jerks his head to one side in Huckles' secret code for break. Blood rushes hotly to Honey's face. He is a boy she could love if her daddy weren't sick, if love could salvage what's lost.

In the frozen section she shoves two packages of phyllo dough deep into the waist pocket of her Mega-Basket apron. She's already stolen the fancy cashews and Greek olives Momma requested but since it's for a wake, she considers it an offering. In the back room, she slides the dough into her backpack and heads for the freezer so it won't go soft before she starts home. She lifts the lever on the heavy metal door to see the familiar sides of meat hanging from giant hooks. Half-pigs, with their white wax skins, make her think of Madame Tussaud's museum. She's never been there but she knows that the figures look almost like real people because she's seen the ones at the Winfield fair: Cher, Marilyn Monroe, Elvis. She has a photo of herself standing plain-faced next to Elvis while her friend Shyla cups the bulging space between his legs and giggles. The night that picture was taken, Shyla met a guy from a neighboring high school behind the Whip-r-Whirl while Honey watched the fireworks explode in the sky, wondering if a person miles and miles away could see what she saw.

Tuna's face appears in the small window of the freezer. He flashes his perfect teeth. Honey drops her backpack on a stool and steps out of the cold, into the break room.

"Hey," says Tuna.

"Hey."

"What you doin' in there?"

"Oh. My mom needs stuff for a wake she's catering tomorrow."

"Cool. You wanna hit it?" He means: *Do you want to smoke*, which she hasn't ever done before because she's afraid she'll go buggy and never be normal again. Her mom plastered stickers from the Reagan-era "Just Say No" campaign in her room when she was a kid. She never could get that last one off her bedside table so it's still the last thing she sees before she turns out the light. Now that sticker seems to reply to all sorts of things that keep her awake at night: did her daddy remember the girl she was before he went to Iraq? Did he have to kill anyone? Did he love her mother anymore?

Her friend Shyla smokes dope but would probably kill Honey if she knew she was thinking about smoking with Tuna. Shyla dates white boys on the football team and she'd give Honey a hard time for wasting a good time with a half-friend, "half-breed." So Honey says, "I just don't wanna be all creeped out when I see my mom, you know?"

"Nah, that's cool. Just come out back with me and chill then. We'll talk."

Outside, they make a place for themselves around the corner from the back door, midway down a stairwell that blocks the wind but still lets in the late June light. They sit just out of view of passers-by and parking lot traffic. Tuna takes out a half-smoked joint, the size of a bullet, and lights it with a Mega-Basket match, shaking it out as he puffs on the joint. Honey watches him enough to take mental notes (*his lips never touch the paper*) but she doesn't want to gape, so she looks toward the heavy metal door. Tuna exhales extending his arm so it rests on his knee.

"You smoke cigarettes?" he asks.

"My dad does. In eighth grade, Shyla and I used to steal them and climb out to Chatty Ridge to watch the traffic and try to smoke."

"It's different than cigarettes, you know?"

"I figure."

"This shit's Mexican brick weed. Kills your lungs but does the trick," he says.

"How do you know it's Mexican?" Honey asks. Tuna is Salvadorian, she knows that somehow. But he could be full of shit so she challenges him because he always seems to know more, or wants to know more, than the rest of the sophomores in her class about lots of things. Like the time he told Mr. Kusick, the physics teacher, that at his grandmother's wake, he watched her spirit lift out of the casket in her purple funeral dress and crash around the house against the stucco ceiling and along the stairwell until someone pulled the hatch to the attic so she could float up there and rub her spirit body against the clothes his mother *hadn't* chosen for her to wear on the day of the viewing. Then she floated out the attic window that was open just wide enough to let the summer heat escape, and spirits, too. "So what's with that and relativity, huh? She went up but she never came down," Tuna said. Half the class laughed and eyed Mr. Kusick thinking *yeah, what about that?* and Mr. Kusick said, "Maybe she hasn't come down just yet." And Tuna shut up.

Tuna says, "I don't *know* that it comes from there, but I figure. I mean all that shit comes up that way, you know? That's what my boys tell me."

"Oh yeah? Which boys?"

"Chino and Hatch and Cooler."

They are mixed too, like him, but in different ways. And they stick together, all of the penitentiary workers' boys because they ride the same bus and come from all over and move like nomads.

"Like they know anything about drug traffic?" Honey scoffs.

"Hatch's dad told him. He does drug offenses at the pen, you know?"

"Oh."

"Hey. Your dad's home, right? Sergeant Berkowski?" He takes another hit, and Honey watches his hairline moving slightly at the temples as he exhales, cut with clippers into his head the way she thought only black people did. "I saw the sign on the Route 15 overpass."

"Yeah. My brother JP did that. Came home about three weeks ago."

"Cool. How long was he there?"

"Three tours. He was gone like five years."

"Is he done?"

"He's home. On leave." She doesn't know the terms of his service. Doesn't even know what his daily duties were or if "leave" is what to call his status. She just knows he came home thin and quiet, missing a leg, carrying a flag folded in a triangle. He'd gone into town with a friend, Abdul, who was killed in the same suicide bombing. The irony of it, standing next to each other, that the Muslim should go. She wonders if her father wishes he had gone too.

"I've got recruiters calling me already," Tuna says.

"You're not even eighteen."

"They don't care. I *will* be next year so they're stacking their cards."

"Would you do that?"

"What?"

"Serve."

"Yeah, why not? Good money. If I wanna go to school when I get back, they'll pay tuition."

"Do you even wanna go to college?"

"Yeah. I'd be the first."

"First to what? First to serve or first to go to college?" She wants to say *first to kill or die for this country?* But she doesn't.

"First to serve *and* go to college. My ma wants me to set an example for my little brothers." He looks proud just saying it.

"Look at you."

"What?"

"They're not calling *my* house."

"You're a girl and you're sixteen."

"So? Girls can serve. Tuna, really. Did you ask Chino and Hatch and the other brown boys if they got a call?"

"What're you saying?"

"Nothing. It's just… don't be a victim of the system, that's all."

"A victim? I'm no victim." He says it cocky, like he's insulted. "I'm taking advantage of a system the government set up to serve and protect people like you."

"For the *people*," Honey says sarcastically.

"Let me ask you this," he says, examining the joint between his thumb and forefinger. "Does your dad think he's a victim?"

She has to think hard about this. She separates her dad into two men: the man he was then and the man he is now. The man in uniform thought bravery was a term for the weak. The man in the upstairs bedroom cries at night when he thinks no one can hear him. He cries, she thinks, for what he's lost—Abdul, his daughter's girlhood, his dignity. Still, she doesn't know how to answer the question. When she went to the base with Momma and JP to pick him up and bring him home, his waist was so small, his pants doubled under his belt, one pant leg pinned primly where his leg was missing. He'd been hospitalized in Baghdad for four months while he healed.

"I don't know if he thinks he's a victim. I don't think so," she says finally because she wants it to be true.

Honey feels him smiling at her from the corner of his eye. He's caught her bullshitting. She's not a real troublemaker, like the ones he spends most of his time with who get in girl fights and swear at their mothers. She's the smart kind, the worst kind. Honey knows she's a pretty girl with teeth that are either alluring or strange because of the gap between the top two. But the teeth themselves are straight and white and she's never had braces. She smiles with her lips closed mostly, because they're full and she hopes with Tuna looking at her from the side like this that she looks pretty to him.

"You live close to here, right?" Tuna asks.

"Yeah. I walk here."

"Like in one of those nice houses on the hill?"

"It's not on the hill. It's up Dell Drive."

"But it's nice."

"I don't know. It's kinda ugly. It's my grandma's old house—she left it to us when she died. Has one of those weird front doors with the vented glass and a chain link fence and my dad never finished the paint job so it's like yellow on the front but brown on the back."

"Sounds all right to me. Everything looks the same on pen grounds—my house and Chino's and Hatch's. All built together just doors on different sides is all." He leans back against the steps so he can look at the sky and tugs back on her elbow so she'll join him too. The clouds are moving fast and changing into big, round puffy things that roll like a movie reel until they're out of sight again. Honey's jeans are tight and low cut and the sliver of flesh between her hipbone and her navel is bare against the hand Tuna lets fall against her. He flicks what's left of the joint and rolls over her, like one of the clouds, moving fast.

"Look at me," he says.

She looks, and as soon as she does, she knows this is it. His eyes are dark and rimmed with red. A wisp of smoke trails from his mouth. He is handsome, a stunner. She concentrates on the details of his head. His haircut makes the skin on his skull seem so thin she can see veins and maybe even the undulations of his brain. She thinks about how clean he seems when she sees him with his boys at school. They all dress the same way in baggy jeans and new, loose-laced Jordans and over-sized white tees with creases down the middle like they're straight from a new package—he and Chino and Hatch all little soldiers of a different army.

"Hey," Tuna says. "*Look* at me."

Now her eyes are fixed on his, his face in close-up goes double image. She puts her hands on either side of that glory-seeking head hoping she might feel what's going on inside. This is the moment she will replay in her mind again and again because this is the moment when she gives in. "Now you're looking," he says, and he kisses her. His tongue inside her mouth tastes like rubber. This is scary and strange and magnificent, for now.

Her skin is hot, her head feels swollen, his hands are working so fast. He slides her jeans and underwear down to her knees, and she stops breathing because everything is in plain light. Her ass is on concrete, making little corrugated dimples there.

"Tuna…" she says.

"Tell me."

She is silent because what's to tell?

"It's okay," he says.

"I don't know if I want to."

"You don't have to." And she realizes that because she has a choice, she wants this even more. Briefly she thinks of Shyla. About how last summer on Chatty Ridge, Shyla told her that Jimmy Riggs couldn't get the condom on because he went soft and freaked out and rubbed her with it instead and that it felt like some big, wet eraser.

Tuna kisses her again and she thinks, *this kiss is slow and soft, it makes a person forget.* And she does. She forgets that this boy is not like her, that this boy will never meet her parents. She is conscious of the light on her skin, wonders how the triangle of hair between her legs must look to him, if he's seen a lot of girls this way, if he thinks she's pretty, not beautiful, just pretty would be enough.

She tries to kiss him like she's admired in the movies, better than anyone she's kissed before, tries to make her kiss into one that would make him forget she's white. His hand is between her legs, then his pelvis is against her and it's like she's being cut with a hot knife. Everything comes into focus all at once. She sits up, knocking Tuna back, his eyebrows forced together by the wrinkle in his brow. He yanks at his pants, so does she. She is so, so sorry and scared. She backs up the steps, staring at him while taking hold of the metal railing to steady herself.

In the freezer, she closes the door behind her and pants big clouds of hot air amid the familiar sides of beef. She smooths her hair and finds her backpack and stands for a long moment in the smell of meat, concentrating on the inside cavity of a cow where she imagines she could curl up. In the break room, Tuna is just coming in as she shuts the freezer door behind her. He looks at the floor.

"I gotta go. My mom's waiting for me," Honey says, conscious already of the way this excuse will sound in her own head later on, maybe even for years to come.

"Can I walk you?"

"No."

"I'd like to see where you live."

She doesn't look at him. "Some time, maybe, but not tonight."

"I'm sorry if…"

"Don't make it like this…" She wants to say, *Don't make me into something you pity*. She shakes her head. "Gotta go," she says, feeling the weight of the door as it closes behind her.

Now she is alone with her thoughts and anticipates the dialogue she will invent with her mother as she watches her dart around the kitchen in her apron or what she will say to her dad when she quietly pushes open the bedroom door. Sometimes she calls Shyla on the way home, to pass the time, so that when she reaches the back door it doesn't feel like she's walked at all. Honey looks back at Mega-Basket. In the darkening sky, the clouds have stopped moving so fast and are hanging above the parking lot like some high school stage curtain waiting to be yanked away. She is sore like the time she fell hard on the balance beam in the seventh grade and it hurt to pee for days afterward. She finds a Burger King napkin in the front pocket of her backpack, surveys the lot and quickly shoves it down her pants, wants to be sure she's not torn, bleeding. The napkin is like sandpaper but the mucous is clear when she brings it up to inspect it.

She heads up Dell Drive, considering what it would be like to have Tuna as a boyfriend. But then she thinks of the way her mother would scrutinize him when he came to the door. And she remembers how stubborn adults can be—maybe just the tone of his skin would remind her daddy of Abdul or even Mrs. Hamza. She doesn't know if that's good or bad. Tuna seemed so comfortable in the stairwell while she felt ugly and awkward. Did he know she's never done it before? Does he think she's a slut? Is he on the phone already to Hatch and Chino and Cooler? She thinks of the vein in his temple under her fingertips. She doesn't know if she's a virgin anymore, or if it matters.

She passes Kim Richter's house where her mother plays Euchre every month and where the front door always sports a seasonal wreath. There's no season right now—it's just summer—but not even that for a few more weeks, so Honey thinks about how normal, for once, the ring of plastic flowers seems with its gaudy purple bow. Still, there's the "Bring our troops home" bumper sticker on the Chevy in the driveway and the "God bless America" flag stuck in the ground by the walkway. Honey wonders if the Richters have done that for her family.

When she arrives at home, she notices a Mega-Basket plastic sack on the front steps. More books from Mrs. Hamza. She considers the house—*is it nice?*—and thinks it could be with a little care—the hedges trimmed back, a fresh coat of paint, a new fence. Honey takes the sack and glances up to the second floor where the light in JP's old room is on. Across the street, the curtains are almost closed except for a swatch of light she realizes now contains the face of a beautiful, dark woman with black hair falling in waves. It's Mrs. Hamza, without her head covering. Honey begins to wave and Mrs. Hamza lets the curtain fall. *Salam(i) I like 'em.*

She walks up the cracking driveway, around back of the house, past the broken lawn mower and through the torn screen door to where her mother, in her apron, works at the stove. From behind, the gray roots of her hair are glaringly, unapologetically exposed. Glass bowls sit on the counter, something boils on the burner, the oven exhales the smell of pot pie.

"Hey, Angel. How was work?"

"Fine. Saw Mrs. Hamza. She must've dropped these off," Honey says, putting the books on the counter.

"I dunno why she keeps bringing us those books."

"For Daddy."

"Well, he's not reading 'em."

"She's trying to help."

"Well, maybe we don't need it."

"It's nice of her, Momma."

"When you see her next tell her to drop off a check then. That's the help we need, not goat pie and war books."

It's hard to tell sometimes when her mother's joking and when she's straight. "I don't know why you can't be nice to her. You treat her like a stranger every time she comes to the door. She's been living across the street for five years."

"She is a stranger. A nosy one. You get the phyllo?" she asks.

"The stuff's like $5.50 a pack." Honey removes the phyllo, olives and cashews from her bag and places them on the counter.

"I'm making sausage cheese triangles for the wake. You wanna help?"

"In a little bit. I want to take a shower. Saw Daddy's light on up there when I came home."

"He's in a mood."

"Did he get up today?"

"When the physical therapist came, he yelled and groaned and swore at her. Then he watched old episodes of *China Beach*."

"Have you talked to him?"

"He doesn't wanna be talked to, Honey. He wants to disappear."

"Momma…"

"Well, he does. And when he decides to act like a human being again, I'm all ears. But, I've been waitin' nearly five years and it's like he's been traded in for spare parts and they're sittin' up there in JP's old room." Her hands squeeze sausages out of their casings into a glass bowl.

"I'll be down in a little bit," says Honey taking the sack of books upstairs into her room. From down the hall comes a flicker of TV light beneath the door to JP's old room.

In the shower, she puts a hand between her legs and feels herself slightly swollen there, thinks of Tuna again and how her mother will never know that this happened because she isn't the kind of mother you talk to. Nor is Shyla's mom, who asks Honey to call her Judy, not Mrs. Warley because it makes her feel old. For a moment she wonders what Tuna's mom and dad are like. If she would know them to see them, which one of them he resembles more, if his mother is proud of him or straight lipped and unmoved like her own. She wonders if, when Tuna speaks to his mother in Spanish, it makes her think of him as a toddler in El Salvador with his sunshine smile, framed by the lips that would make him "Tuna," the same lips Honey guesses will soon betray her, the same Antonio who will fight a war on behalf of a country he feels has offered his family so much.

Honey dresses, towels her hair dry and runs a brush through it. She sits on the bed unknotting the plastic sack from Mrs. Hamza. Inside, she finds *Jarhead*, *The Things They Carried*, and *Tuck Everlasting*, which is oddly familiar. The public library still uses a card checkout system, and she flips open the back cover to read the names on the sign-out card. On the first of the two cards are names from the nineties, a few of which she recognizes: Carl Kimbel (moved away in seventh grade), Jody Stackler (whose brother broke his neck jumping off a trestle summer before last), and herself, Honey Berkowski (written just *Honey B*). She remembers *Tuck Everlasting*—a book about a magic spring that grants eternal life—and thinks about the Tucks and what people will do to keep from dying but also to keep from living their lives.

Down the hall, she hears her father talking to the TV in a soft voice that comes through the door with a gurgling sound like water on rocks. When she pushes open the door, she will ask him about what happened, about Abdul, what he remembers of her before the war. That's how she will learn the answer to Tuna's question.

Inside, her father is propped up on pillows, he leans against the headboard of JP's old bed drinking a Budweiser. He looks older with his unshaved beard, silver in the unsteady light of the TV. He turns to her as if he were expecting someone or something else.

"Honey Bee," he says.

"Hey, Daddy. How you feeling?"

"Oh, okay, I guess. Whatcha got?" He puts down the empty can.

"Mrs. Hamza dropped these books off." She crawls up onto the bed and stretches her legs out parallel to her father's. She notices that the white blanket outlines his legs: one longer than hers, the other thick and knotted like firewood. He catches her looking at his changed body and pulls at the blanket to distract her.

"War stories, huh?"

"Not all of them." She shows him *Tuck Everlasting*. "This one's about people who live forever."

He grunts. "You wanna read to me?" He says it like he means *everyone wants to do something*. "And my choices are war stories or fairy tales?"

"We don't have to read," she says.

"Either kind, they've all got sad endings."

Honey puts the books down while her father pulls another beer from the plastic rings.

"Why don't you tell *me* a story?" she says.

"What kind?"

"Tell me about Abdul."

"That's not a story. That's a person." He is silent for a long time while Archie Bunker sits at his kitchen table listening to Ethel carve away at his nerves the way older people do.

Honey wonders if this is the right way to get him to look at her. She thinks too, if, when he does, she'll look different to him: different than before the war and different than this morning, before she went to work, before Tuna and the stairwell. *Salaam Alaikum, peace be unto you*, she thinks.

Honey is busy picking at the fringe of the blanket, her mind at work but lost to him. Can he know her thoughts? She is sixteen, a woman with responsibilities she does not even know she bears. She lays her head against his bony shoulder and her wet hair reveals the scar there. She wants him to trace it with his fingers, wants him to tell her he hasn't forgotten. Instead, he takes Honey's hand in his and with his free hand rolls the bedspread down around the lumpy stump of his leg, wrapped in white gauze, aching more in the dim light of the room and the silence between them. He takes her hand with its fingernails bitten back, their chipping polish, places it where his leg no longer is, where it ends.

He says, "Feel this."

Cicadas

Perhaps Corinne has had three by the time her daughter brings over her homework with a smudgy, photocopied image looking only like an inkblot. It takes Corinne's reading glasses and some interpretation to understand the image itself—a cicada emerging from the unsuspicious earth.

Lucille says, "I need to know what they sound like."

Lucille is seven, a girl whose curiosities, at least for the time being, are confined to the behaviors of others, so her mother is eager to oblige her interest. Lucille tells her mother that the cicadas are coming, that her teacher, Ms. Landry, has told them the sound is deafening. Lucille widens her eyes frightfully when she says "deafening," which prompts Corinne to take another long sip. Lucille's assignment is to make a prediction about what they will sound like. She has written: *The cicaydas will sownd umazed. Like when you see somthing for the first time. Ever.*

Corinne flips open the laptop and navigates to YouTube where she selects a BBC segment on cicadas. The sound begins immediately—a siren-like buzzing, electric, persistent. It's David Attenborough narrating—a haunting whisper in the darkness, explaining the insects' emergence, their ascent up the trees whose root sap has nourished them for seventeen years. The two watch as a mature cicada splits its shell and arches its creamy body. The wings unfurl like small scrolls revealing intricate river maps. Without recognizing their own phenomena, they leave behind their larval casings by the millions—candy wrappers at the base of the trees. Corinne and Lucille's jaws slacken with amazement and when it's over, the two watch again, and then finally one last time so that Corinne has finished her drink and Lucille's dreams will be milky with orchestral bug music.

The vodka is nearly gone, she might as well. The dog needs to be walked. The baby who has been stacking Tupperware at their feet while they've watched the computer, even as he's turned his ear to the sound of the buzzing the way a dog might, needs a diaper change. She should beckon her middle child from the couch, remind him that too much television rots the brain. But he has not asked for anything in an hour and she is enjoying feeling in low demand. She considers dinner as she stirs her drink. There is something they should be preparing for. She had this thought even before the cicadas, but now she's even more distracted by the bugs, by the baby, by her own vices, to remember. She checks the wall calendar but finds nothing scheduled. Ted phones to tell her he's minutes away and she chooses not to ask him what she might be missing, given that she's the keeper of the schedule. Corinne puts a pot of water on the stove. Even if she hasn't decided what she'll cook, a pot of water is useful. Pasta. Vegetables. A few hot dogs.

Now, she lays the baby on the floor for a diaper change while Lucille hollers from her room about the location of her yellow tutu. Lucille wears leotards and tutus most of the time when she's not in school. It makes her look fancy and graceful and, as of yet, does not interfere with her curious investigations of others' lives and habits.

Ted is home now and Corinne pours the remainder of her drink into a travel mug and heads out the door with the dog. If her life afforded her a routine, she could consider this dog-walking part of it. She'd like more of that, the way

Ted has one—up at six, out the door by seven, a little CNN online before he cranks out the requisite emails of the day. But, on this particular day, for this half hour, and when she's alone, she relishes the escape—to leave the kids and their demands and the laundry in the dryer and the mail untouched. To leave even her husband so she could fantasize about what a return might look like, his sidelong grin, his welcoming arms that would say, *I didn't know if you'd be back.*

The sun is low but strong and spring's colors are at their peak. The last of the tulips are closed tightly for the evening, the flowering pears are dropping their petals like a storm. The sidewalk is moving swiftly beneath her stride. Tinker doesn't even strain against the leash when they pass Jade, the neighborhood golden asleep on the sidewalk in front of the corner lot. Jade's eyelids are twitching ever so slightly with the stuff of dreams. Across the street, a man throws a softball with his daughter. That daughter is named for a season, though the name escapes her, even as the father calls across the street and waves. Corinne waves in response. That man once spent a winter morning in her kitchen when he'd locked the keys in his car and she'd offered him coffee while he waited for AAA to arrive. That's when she'd learned the name of this girl, even remembered that she had topped both coffees off with Baileys while he explained to her the origin of that name.

Tinker has scrunched up his rear-end in preparation for a squat. She looks away to preserve Tinker's humility. She inspects the Target bag in her hand for holes. It's the ones from the grocery store and the drug store that always seem to be riddled with holes. Bending to scoop it up, the light seems to flip, she can see it on the backs of her eyelids and she has to put the tips of her fingers down in the grass to steady herself before she can stand up again.

Now she is passing the park where the boy who once fell from the monkey bars is sitting with his mother. She is always well-dressed and has impeccable manners and has a tendency to clap in her child's direction when she believes the child is in jeopardy of hurting someone or himself. Since Corinne has no children with her today, she can offer a wave and walk on. It's then that she realizes she's forgotten her phone. And it's then that she realizes how much of a relief that provides. She would text Ted to let him know about the boiling water, about the thing she thinks she may have forgotten. She doesn't give Ted enough credit for being self-sufficient, a terrific father, the first person to pour her a drink after his day at the office. If she had her phone, she'd call him to tell him how much she appreciates him right now. Ted can handle things. She can picture him—the baby riding "pinky back," brandishing the misplaced tutu, a bag of mixed vegetables already in the boiling water.

And because she knows he's got it all figured out, she walks on. Her cup is empty. She walks into town the long way, past the high school where the color guard is practicing their half-time routine, past the market where the boy named Tony has always been kind to her, always carries her groceries to the car, always calls her ma'am which makes her feel a little older than she thinks she looks, past the dog park that's muddy from recent rain, into town where the door of the fire station is open and the men are enjoying the glory of a late spring day. The red trucks gleam brightly.

Downtown, which is the kind of town where there is one drinking establishment, one decent Thai restaurant and a dozen hair salons, she notices the swinging windows of the tavern are open to the sidewalk. There is a place in the window that would be perfect for watching the sun grow shadows into darkness. Tinker can rest outside while she has just one more.

She pulls a stool close to the window between a man she knows she's seen before and two women with white wine interrupting each other's sentences. Corinne orders the usual:

a vodka soda with lots of lime. Once it's gone she orders another and inspects the thin red straw in her glass, curious how it's all gone up the straw and down the hatch so quickly. Tinker has laid down in the dirt, exposing his belly to the now nearly faded sun.

"You live in the red house on Blanchard, right?" says a voice from the side. She's been looking at her wristwatch in an effort to figure out how long she's been gone from home.

He asks again. "Blanchard road?"

She swivels her stool just enough to suggest she'll talk. "Blanchard. Yes. You?"

"No. Not Blanchard."

She's surrendered a personal detail and realizes he hasn't done the same. "How do you know?"

"I've seen your dog in the street. That's him there, right?" He points to Tinker who has scratched himself a nest in the dirt.

"That's Tinker, yes." Dammit. She's done it again.

"I'm Randy."

She's wise now. "Hi, Randy," she says without reciprocating. She's only halfway through her second drink. If she sips faster, she'll look tacky. She remembers that there's a payphone in the back. She places her napkin over her glass and excuses herself.

When she picks up the receiver, the dial tone reminds her of the cicadas. It buzzes so persistently that she waits slightly too long before she dials the home number. No one answers. She tries Ted's cell but he's turned it off. Goes straight to voicemail. "Ted, it's me. Just calling to say I took an extra-long walk. I'll be home real soon. Gorgeous night. Love you."

It's the pursuit of the sound of the cicadas that draws her back outside. What might they sound like? They just might sound *umazed*. She abandons her second drink, abandons Randy and his probing small talk. She's back on the sidewalk, liquor in her legs, Tinker tugging at the leash after his rest in the dirt. She's walking in search of a sound. Her daughter says they're coming, her daughter's teacher says they're coming. She remembers the last time they'd come, now too long ago to really remember her age accurately. It was summer, the Fireman's Carnival just across the street from her childhood home. Before she and her sister went out to stuff themselves with french fries and funnel cakes, before they spent their last quarters on the steeple chase and the Whip-r-Whirl, they had gone out to the common oak in their back yard and found the cicada casings littering the ground. Brownish, transparent husks whispering like cellophane beneath their treading feet. No one had told them they were coming, and though she doesn't remember the anticipation, she remembers feeling cheated that she'd missed their arrival and performance—that she had been left only with their remains.

Sometimes she's driving the car, she glances at the clock, she's been driving for miles but can't recall the route. There must've been stop lights and stop signs and traffic laws by which to have abided. But there is no memory. No memory of whether she slowed the car down or plowed right through, if there had been an angry person waving a clenched fist in her direction, an endangered child or dog stepping back onto the curb as she raced through red lights and crosswalks. And when she comes to consciousness, it's like clawing back from a dream. You were somewhere else and now you are not. The somewhere else is already lost and sometimes more important than the place you are going. Sometimes it's only now that's important.

Here's her daughter's elementary school. Brown bricks and floor to ceiling glass on the new addition. The sun is so low in the sky that the orange tube slide seems to glow. The parking lot is full and a wall of light cuts across a row of cars. There is her husband's car. And there are two parents scrambling for the door. It's the flowers in the woman's hands that trigger the recall. Lucille is dancing. It's what she's forgotten. Like how she's gotten here, like the red lights and the stop signs and later, she'll realize, like her children's first days of school and her husband's shoe size. She will even forget that her daughter brought her the picture of the cicadas that looked like an inkblot. She'll remember how she spelled *umazed* and the droning sound, the persistence, the hypnotic lull and the remains.

For now, she's on the heels of the latecomers, rushing into the auditorium with such haste she feels incapable of being quiet. The hot breath of stage lights and nervous bodies fills the space in her throat where words might be. She is dizzy and once her eyes adjust to the darkness, she sees Lucille, center left, one of a dozen buttercups in yellow tulle and tights encircling the fairy princess. The music fades and dies so quickly she isn't able to determine the song, the composer. Lucille has been humming that tune all week.

Now the dancers form two lines to curtsy and the applause begins, Corinne's own hands leaden at her sides. Even from this distance she can tell her daughter is scanning the faces in the front row, discovering her mother is not there. She has missed it: the performance and the possibility. Now, the buttercups part and the fairy princess sails to the front of the stage, her adolescent legs rippling with muscle. Lucille watches intently as the princess cups a delicate hand to her heart and curtsies. And then, in unison, the buttercups raise their fleshy arms like wings and draw their hands across their own hearts. She is trying to be as graceful as she can, long before a time when she might be. And Corinne is left without anticipation, only its wake. Left only with her small girl, her hand on heart, no sound of cicadas approaching.

The Dwindling

Marlene's daughter, Tess, at a distance, appeared self-assured, fluid and cheerful. Tess engaged with the girls who flanked her, one dark, one light, gesticulating with her hands, charming them with her storytelling, her inventive use of body language. There, in the minivan, how fortunate Marlene felt to bear witness—her daughter the sun, her new friends unknown planets in her orbit.

A black SUV slid in front of the girls, eclipsing the scene and engulfing the friends, then slid past again, leaving Tess alone on the curb. Her face, once animated, was blank. Marlene watched Tess retrieve her phone from the pocket of her oversized, pink shag coat and tap out a text:

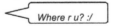

Marlene's phone dinged as she watched her daughter freeze and suspend in time—a brief, distorted glitch—Tess in pixelated colors. Her jaw froze and set, her eyes and shoulders caught in a momentary seizure before animating again. (Was it a figment? A visual error?) And then, just as quickly, she returned to her original form—sun kissed skin, freckles on the bridge of her nose, ears like pale apricots, a small hoop in each. Weeks ago, when she'd witnessed this for the first time, she'd thought she'd imagined it. Marlene drew a fast breath and replied:

> Right here. Look up.

When she did, there was no brightness of recognition, no gratitude, no aftereffects. Just a blank face and the headstrong bustling of big coat and bags charging toward the van. The van's door unlocked with a heavy metal chug and Tess climbed in.

"Hey, babe. You feeling ok?"

"Yeah. Fine. Why?"

Marlene avoided explanation. "How was the movie?"

"Meh."

"Funny?"

"Not particularly."

"Adam Sandler and not funny?"

Tess shrugged.

Marlene sat at the light on Broadway, her left turn signal rhythmic in the silence. She inventoried her daughter, looking hard for signs of physical change, put the back of her hand gently to her daughter's warm face.

"Mom. I'm fine." Tess tapped furiously into her phone. The days were getting shorter and the blue evening was approaching.

"Did you have fun with those new girls at least? Remind me of their names?"

"Scarborough and Layla."

"Scarborough. Interesting. That's different. Is she... are either of them Tech-Gen?"

Tess rolled her eyes. "I didn't ask them... geez."

"Tess. It's not a secret, right? They know you're...?"

"No. They don't. I'd like to keep it that way."

Marlene sighed. "I'm sorry." Her apologies seemed to come in a repetitive loop these days.

"I don't want to talk about it all the time the way you do."

"I don't want to talk about it all the time. But I don't think it's something to be ashamed of."

"High school is already hard enough. I don't need them thinking I'm a freak."

The sun, lowering itself toward the horizon, sent rays through the clouds like extra-terrestrial superhighways. Marlene changed the subject. "Look at that, Tess. Beautiful!" She gestured to the sky.

Tess glanced briefly, her face illuminated by the glow of her screen. "Love."

They had a rule about phones in the car but tensions were high at home, and Marlene had hoped she wouldn't have to remind her.

Tess continued her tapping.

"Tess."

"What?"

"The rule…"

"About phones when we're driving."

"Right."

"And when we're at the table. And no double screen-time and none at homework time and…" she contorted her voice into a Siri-like adaptation.

"I don't sound like that." Marlene said.

"Maybe I wish you did."

"You wish I sounded like Siri?" she joked.

"I said maybe. God."

At the intersection, a young father in a black knit beanie pushed a stroller with one hand and held a small dog by the leash in the other. Marlene wondered if this man was sent out before dinner by a partner, a wife, for some time out of his/her hair while s/he cooked dinner, took a bath, exercised. There would be no such partner at home when she and Tess arrived. The car was hers, the house, the dog to walk, the food to prepare, the child to raise. All hers. Tess was among the first generation of Tech-Gen kids, as they'd been referred to, born of woman and Artificial Intelligence, no sperm required, no intimate relationship, no physical partner with whom to bear out one's days, to argue about the relative costs/ benefits of limiting screen time, organic foods, private school options.

"Too young," interjected Tess, seeing Marlene's eyes on the man.

"I wasn't considering him that way. Geez, Tess. He's probably not even thirty!"

Tess made a face. Smug.

Marlene had first considered a Tech-Gen pregnancy after years of a barren partner landscape. There had been occasional charming prospects but few with whom she could fathom a real sense of longevity. There had been Brent, whom she never failed to call Brett or even Brit, which was undoubtedly a turn-off but which she simply could not rewire her brain to correct. There had been Nico who was bright and very fashionable but too measured and unforgiving to be a good partner let alone a father. The most recent had been Uri, who was playful and spontaneous, extra wild in bed and she'd figured these attributes made it such that he'd have been proud to be a stud in her childbearing project, as long as it meant the results weren't restrictive to him. One evening, after they'd smoked pot and made love and were playing Scrabble in the nude, she'd asked him. Just said it outright—*What if I said you'd be great DNA for a father, but you don't have to be one?* He'd let his drink perspire on the table and he wiped at the ring as he spoke, *Who says I don't want to be one?* And that had been its own dealbreaker—Marlene failing to see him in his own image.

"Don't you want a partner?" Tess asked earnestly.

"I thought I did, yeah. But I'm too busy now."

"Too busy? Or too tired?"

"I don't know. Both." Marlene forced a laugh.

"Mom, you're like, still pretty. Still young enough."

"Oh, thanks hon." Marlene grimaced. "I've got lots of friends, companions. I don't need a partner right now."

"What about Tom?"

Marlene had known Tom since she'd moved to Boston after college. He'd been cutting her hair that long—had seen it through a pixie stage, bangs, through highlights and balayage. He had held her hand through multiple rounds of fruitless IVF, counseled her through Uri and finally offered his own sperm for insemination, though Marlene refused, admittedly harboring concerns about his ambition. But she was also embarrassed to realize, just then, that Tom was probably her closest friend.

"Tom is a friend. He cuts my hair. He cuts *your* hair now too. Sometimes, we go out afterwards and get Mai Tais." Marlene didn't tell Tess that he could've been the father.

"Sounds like a date."

"Not a date. Two un-partnered people drinking Mai Tais. And, I'm not sure he isn't just fascinated by my story. Our story."

"Tech-Gen?"

"Yeah."

The procedure had been relatively simple. In a unique and experimental program vetted by some of the world's top doctors and researchers, healthy women of childbearing age could be screened to qualify for a Tech-Gen pregnancy. After meeting physical benchmarks, women were selected to have a port installed in the abdomen—via a small incision to the left of, and on the same meridian as, the belly button. And then, when the time was right, the woman could book her appointment to download digital DNA via her port with something barely more complex than a USB cord. The first generation was coming of age, while at the previous month's Tech-Gen Summit, they had reported two hundred new national births, putting the total number of Tech-Gen kids at roughly ten thousand. Appointments were scarce and coveted. It was partnership with oneself. It was the first of its kind.

"We *are* weirdos," said Tess.

"Not really. Anything that subverts the dominant paradigm is always perceived as weird."

"Is that what the sociologists say?" Tess continued to peck at her phone while participating in the mockery.

"They do, actually. Did you even listen at the last Summit?"

"Kind of."

Sometimes, Marlene felt a kind of sizzling at the port site, even some fifteen years later when she ran her fingers over the small rectangle of tissue on her belly that bore no Cesarian scars, no linea nigra, but the scar of a socio-technological experiment she still occasionally boasted about to friends who went the route of natural conception. A cadre of single mothers had emerged, bonded by their experience, their fortitude and independence. While the Tech-Gen mothers knew their children surely carried their own litany of challenges, the whole lot of them had each other. The program guaranteed community through a series of regular summits used to glean data, to celebrate and commiserate, to humanize their half-human pregnancy and normalize their parenting journey. There would be cheese. Wine. Some kind of TedX speaker harvested from the realm of psychology, science, the human experience.

"Where is the Tech-Gen Summit this time?" Tess asked wearily, finally looking up from her phone.

"Copley. Boston Public Library."

"Books. Great. Lemme guess. We'll watch a documentary together."

"It's a beautiful landmark, Tess, with enough space for all of us to gather. And I'm not even sure what the topic is this time. Who the speaker is. I just skimmed the email."

"Email," Tess scoffed. She scrolled through Metaverse and landed on the Tech-Gen group. "Why doesn't Tech-Gen migrate to Repo, or even Tik-Tok would be better. God. It's so old school. No wonder attendance is dwindling."

"It's only once a month, Tess. And attendance is dwindling, because, well…"

"Because people are saying our *population* is dwindling." Tess rolled her eyes dismissively. It haunted Marlene that what might be something to which they should lend significant attention was disregarded so easily by her daughter.

Marlene had joined a chat room years ago that connected Tech-Gen mothers from across the northeast, where the children of the Tech-Gen experiment were the oldest. But new mothers seemed to dominate the online landscape now: mothers of infants and six year olds, mothers who lived as far away as Albuquerque and Seattle who prattled on about feeding times and diaper rash, about first foods and sore breasts. And new subgroups had formed, born out of fear and inquiry after a spate of incongruous deaths of Tech-Gen teenagers that had the community shaken.

> I know a mom @GenMom28 whose daughter is very sick right now and dr's are stumped how to treat… rapid weight loss, respiratory infection, subcutaneous discoloration

> Who in the Boston area has used Dr. Rikkar for Tech-Gen repro? Wondering if we share similar experiences. DM me.

> DMing. Do NOT recommend.

> Not an issue of individual doctor. My son, 15, is fine so far, but I'm terrified. Technology is not fully vetted and we are first generation lab rats…

> Has nothing to do with the media. In fact, I wouldn't be surprised if they've been "hushed."

> Tech-Gen is a modern miracle. I am so thankful. I've got a Healthy and incredible 14-year-old. The "tragedies" that have befallen some Tech-Gen kids are like those that might befall any "normally" conceived kiddo. The media's blowing things out of proportion.

> Reddit thread: #TheDwindling

Marlene's own consultation with her Tech-Gen doctors, whom she closely trusted, was both honest and inconclusive. They admitted there had been an uncomfortable number of recent deaths which puzzled them. The internet and social media swirl knit together a pattern that suggested Tech-Gen kids might become terminal around age sixteen. Rema Larinski had been a girl they'd met through the summits who'd recently passed away of a complication the experts and doctors were still attempting to understand. Her death had been sudden and alarming, the veins under her skin blackening in her final days until it looked as though she'd been wrapped in fishing nets. Marlene had phoned the mother who was distraught and sent dinner and lilies with a note that read, "May the passage of time and memories of Rema stitch up your wounded heart." Tess had barely blinked. Was it Tech-Gen that accounted for this lack of affect? Was Tess too digital, not human enough? Marlene couldn't be sure.

"Does it concern you? The new buzz about the population? Do you read about it?" Marlene asked.

"Not really. What could I do about it anyway? They'll tweak an upgrade and it'll be fine. We don't even know if it's a thing yet."

Marlene did admire Tess's ability to defer the anxiety that so easily plagued her. "Do you think about Rema?"

Tess clicked and swiped her phone and in an instant, Rema filled the screen—her nose scrunched, her pink tongue clamped between white teeth, her two fingers raised in a peace sign. Tess flashed the bright image in Marlene's face.

"Yeah. Rema." Marlene smiled. It was comforting to see the smooth visage of her face as Marlene remembered it, not as she imagined it looked in death.

"Temporary, right?" Tess replied as the minivan swirled around the rotary and entered 93, the Tetris-like skyline disappearing in the gray clouds above it. "Isn't that what we learn? Like in these summits? It's all just temporary?" Marlene was disoriented—was Tess appeasing her or parroting back what concerned her about Tech-Gen: the pace of it all belying the permanence Tech-Geners hoped to gain by building an on-line following, a new record-breaking number of likes and shares, a notoriety that made YouTube channels the source of serious income. In the corner of her eye, Marlene glimpsed Tess freeze and smudge, caught between two expressions—one of cynicism, one of disdain, like a Zoom participant caught in unfortunate limbo because of a bad internet feed.

Marlene panicked and counted. *One Mississippi.* "TESS!" *Two Mississippi.* "TESS!?" she shouted, clutching her arm.

"WHAT?! Geez!" Tess sputtered back to life.

When Marlene glanced back, Tess was fluid again, supple. "You just kind of ... you just get quiet."

Tess put a soft hand on Marlene's thigh. "I'm ok, Mom! What's wrong with you today?"

Now Marlene was confused. Was it too much work and not enough sleep? Too much time spent in the conspiracy of the chatroom after learning of The Dwindling? But now this glitch, first observed several weeks ago around Tess's fifteenth birthday, had happened twice in this hour alone.

"I'm sorry. You…" If Marlene explained, would it frighten Tess? Would it awaken her from her disregard? Was what Marlene observed an illness? An anticipated technological condition the doctors might be able to explain? She would call them first thing.

"I… what, Mom?"

"You… leave me."

"What are you talking about? I'm just distracted. Tired. Like you, right?"

Tess was right. It wasn't yet time to be hysterical. Tess hadn't had so much as a sniffle growing up. Maybe this was a manifestation of a common cold, a headache, her menstrual cycle. Maybe it was normal teenage development expressed as some glitch in the algorithmic DNA. Maybe Tess was programmed for this.

"Ok." Marlene wasn't going to say *I'm sorry* this time. "You said *temporary*. Our existence, sure. It must be temporary. But maybe we need to be focused on meaningful ways of permanence."

"You want me to get a job."

How easily she and her daughter misunderstood one another. How opaque she felt Tess could be. "No…" Marlene replied, baffled. "I mean, if you want." She was annoyed. "That's not the point."

"But then why are you so desperate for me to make some lasting impression in a format that constantly changes anyway?"

"This isn't a format, Tess. This is your life."

"But I'm part machine, right? Algorithms and code?"

"That doesn't mean you aren't capable of making meaning!"

The two were at an impasse. The Mystic River, visible on the other side of northbound traffic, twinkled ostentatiously in the diminishing sun, gloating. It was a river made meaningful by mobsters and criminals, by Sean Penn. At the Leverett Connector, finally, she steered the car on to the ramp, stared at the Boston Garden that was hosting Swae Lee in a month's time. Given all the guesses in the world, Marlene would not be able to name one song by Swae Lee.

Finally through the tunnel, they were adjacent to the Esplanade, the long strip of green between Storrow Drive and the Charles River, old trees hanging their long limbs protectively above runners and dog walkers, coeds and parents pushing their strollers. There was the playground she'd taken Tess to for years as a young girl—after every annual checkup at MGH and every autumn before the marathon. She saw the queue for the zipline and the faux rock sculpture covered with brightly dressed children. "Tess."

Tess's face was blue again in the light of her screen. "Mom."

"Do you remember this place?"

Tess glanced up and watched the children briefly, a small cast of familiarity shading her face. "Yeah. I love this place."

"You do?"

"Yeah. That zipline was the best."

Marlene thought about how children like Tess were dying. About how her social/technological experiment might be selling her out. About Rema. "Should we go?" Marlene asked.

"Now?"

"Yeah. Why not?"

"We'll miss the summit."

Marlene shrugged. Truth was, she was feeling uneasy about the summit. Now that she considered it, were the experts and Ted Talkers going to report about The Dwindling? Did she even trust them to keep their participants abreast of new research and development? Start confirming with evidence and anecdotes what some parents of Tech-Gen kids were already experiencing? Marlene felt a wave of nausea.

"Am I too old?" Tess asked.

"Never."

They parked and crossed the Fiedler Footbridge which resembled a cement skateboard ramp or a less elegant Guggenheim structure held high above Storrow stuffed with rush hour traffic. There was the Hatch Shell and the massive sweep of green where proper patriots spread their blankets to watch the symphony play every July 4th, synchronized with the fireworks exploding in the sky.

When they arrived at the edge of the playground, Marlene and Tess watched as the children swirled and mingled, lobbed in the air on swings, crawled the faux rock mound that once seemed monstrous to Tess. It was still fifteen or twenty feet in the air, but a fraction of the size it had once seemed. Parents stood at the base, spotting the youngest climbers, being sure to guide them about where to place a hand, where to secure a foothold. Marlene considered how different it felt to watch these parents, with their hyper-sensitivity, their intentional, nonchalant park clothes, trendy sneakers and five dollar coffees. Their chatter and impressing laughs.

"Zipline?" Marlene asked Tess.

Tess considered it from her place on the wood chips, the children and young parents and au pairs ignoring them, a delightfully odd space in which to be anonymous. With a quick, dismissive shrug, Tess climbed the structure handily and grabbed the rope. Marlene retrieved her phone from her back pocket and swiped quickly for a photo. Tess's face was still full with possibility: bright, expectant. Her limbs were long and knobbed at the joints, still waiting for the full weight of womanhood. When she leapt from the platform, she had to torque her body in an effort to clear the platform so as not to drag her length across it. And, as she launched and the cable gave in to her weight, she was forced to draw her knees to her chest to avoid dragging her feet along the ground. This was the photo Marlene snapped—Tess, her long body balled, the cable sagging under her weight, a wide smile wedged on her face.

"Send that pic to me, I'll add it to my stories," Tess said as she slid open her phone. Marlene noticed how Tess seemed to come alive, to brighten in almost every way as she interacted with apps and images, with the algorithmic language of her heart. Marlene both admired the possibilities and disdained its rule on her.

"Tess…"

"Fine." She clicked her phone closed and put it back in her pocket. "Swings?"

They sat down, side by side, and inventoried the waning crowd. So many families with two partners, mothers and fathers, a nanny in sweatpants and clogs rasping at the children in her German accent. Marlene and Tess gave in to gravity—the weightlessness at the peak and whoosh as their bodies compressed through the lowest valley of the swing. They tried the see-saw and the monkey bars, the slide and the fire pole. One round through each of the features like playground dilettantes, and when they were finished they took a seat on the wall and smiled at one another as the park cooled down.

Finally, they started in the direction of their car, past the last few climbers on the rocky mountain when they heard a sound like a tennis ball to the gut—a hollow, unanticipated sound. Tess and Marlene turned their heads in unison, as if on a line, like marionettes, their mouths slackening as they witnessed it: a boy frozen mid-climb, as if struck by lightning, his forearms seizing and pixelating. Time moved slow, slower. His profile went geometric, his small hands turned to blocks. His face and hair smeared to cubes of peach and yellow, the parting of his mouth grotesque and primitive, the blues of his eyes streaking like short comets.

He was falling backwards in their sightline, his upper half keening toward the ground. Marlene thought about death before anything else. It told her to run toward the falling boy, to get there before she could determine whether a person falling from such a height at such an angle would tolerate the impact, or if the blocks that seemed to compose him might explode to pixels upon contact with the ground.

And Marlene nearly made it—lunging forward with outstretched arms as if she might catch him. The boy's mother, turned away, didn't notice the way his jacket fluttered at the edges as he fell. When the mother finally turned, she would see a stranger descending on her boy. She would see what instinct looks like. Marlene and Tess watched the blur of him bounce on the rubberized surface. His eyes were closed. He did not shatter into flesh-colored pixels. The impact itself seemed to jar him back to flesh and bone. His hair—longer, blond, shagging as it did upon impact—was sweaty at the root. It stuck to his sideburns and separated at his hairline.

The mother crumbled to her boy's side, her face twisting with questions. She feared touching him, her abstract, glitched-out boy. Marlene could feel, on her knees, the warmth of the earth through her corduroys.

"What's happening to him?" Tess pleaded.

The mother gazed up, held Tess's eyes in her own, condemning the question as she asked it of herself.

The boy's face began to soften, shimmered to life, his hands normalizing, separating to distinct fingers and finally, cuticles and fingernails. The mother tipped his head toward her, laid an ear towards his mouth to check for breath.

"Mom?!" Tess demanded, her eyes flooding with tears.

Marlene took hold of the mother's forearm, her orange coat so soft beneath her hand. Marlene wanted to tell her not to move the boy's neck, to tell her he would be fine, but she couldn't be sure she wasn't lying.

"Is he Tech-Gen?" Marlene whispered to the mother.

The woman nodded hyper-fast, her face dissolving to grief. Tess covered her mouth with her hands. Beneath them, her lips were trembling. The boy coughed, his eyes returning to blue points while his mother gathered him to her chest saying, "Elliot, Elliot…"

Tess watched as the final pixels dissipated: teeth, eyelashes, freckles, a light blue vein beneath the thin skin at his temple. Tess's heart seemed to dim in her chest.

"Mom?!" She whispered at Marlene. "He's like me?"

Marlene averted her eyes, looked deeply into the well of the mother's face, her orange coat casting a golden hue in the curve of her bare neck, searched her eyes for wonder and new knowing. Marlene's port scar sizzled and burned and when she took hold of her abdomen to soothe it, she could find no relief.

Small Secrets

Howard found the shoes most fascinating—the variety, the spectrum of styles and materials: sling back, open toe, wedge, bootie, suede, patent, linen, brocade. His mother was a size six narrow, devoted to keeping the boxes and organizing by season. As a child, he'd played in her closet, stepping into a pair of gold lamé mules, putting on her silk robe and leaving it beltless to trail behind him like a waterfall. His mother had emptied a dresser drawer and had filled it with discarded rings, missing clip-ons, broken chains, and antique pins. Upon returning from school, Howard raced to the drawer, slipped a ring over a chubby knuckle, draped chains and beads over his school uniform, and played queen. Occasionally, when he was summoned to the dinner table, he forgot to remove a necklace, an earring, and his mother would discreetly gesture so that Howard would quickly remove it before Mr. Diller noticed.

When Howard's brother, Pat, started off to school, Howard was left at home with his mother who found a kind of forlorn friendship in him—a friendship which sated her rescuing instinct and perhaps offered her temporary redemption from her own self-loathing. In her bedroom, she would create a canopy of clean white sheets still warm out of the dryer (*They can't have wrinkles, can they, Howard? No, sir. Not for us.*), tie one to the canopied bed, another to the ceiling fan until the room was ensconced in cotton sheets caught in the breeze of open windows. She would put on a record, glide through the room hung with sails, keeping her neck long and her chin up until the needle crackled through the dust and picked up the first track. She would take him by the hands, dance him around, hold him to her bosom. And sometimes she'd do the Jitterbug. Howard might've learned his steps from her, might've learned just how to jive right on the balls of his feet and pop his heels and allow his legs to go akimbo. They would collapse on the bed and she would tickle him to tears until he would try on the British accent he'd learned because they spent other afternoons in the little theater downtown watching foreign films and he'd say in a protracted, but nevertheless convincing accent, "Please, Mummy. Please." She would relent and laugh proudly at her happy boy.

Occasionally, when she'd already gotten into the brandy and it was winter and it would take a wee bit longer for Howard's brother or father to arrive home in the evening, she might place a forearm beneath his knees and another behind his head and scoop him up like a baby, too big to be carried this way, and place him on the bench of the vanity. She would continue the ruse, crafting the words in her own British accent, "Sir, how can I be of service?" And Howard, looking down at the silver tray of curious lady-things (a silver-plated brush and comb and a hand-held mirror), was most excited by the peculiars: an eyelash curler, tweezers, an assortment of pots and cremes. He would freeze. He could not ask. But his mother knew. She sensed that his fascination ran deeper than these afternoons. And so his mother would start in with the big puff of powder that smelled like lilacs (a smell he's never stopped missing) and ghost his face with it. She might twist the tube of lipstick, too, dab a red dot on his lower lip to bring some color back to his face. He adored this ritual and felt closer to his mother than ever before, the two of them with their make-up and their small secrets, his mother with her brandy.

Across the street from the Dillers lived Lorne and Sheila Butterman. Lorne worked long days as an attorney at the firm his wife, Sheila, had established, twentieth century woman that she was. On weekday mornings, when Sheila put on a freshly dry-cleaned suit and backed her Mercedes out of the driveway, she waved to the mothers at the bus stop, so coiffed at this early hour, all of them looking well-rested as they waited with their children who were immaculately dressed, their lunches tucked in with notes of encouragement.

After several years of indecision about starting a family and occasional, apathetic sex, Lorne and Sheila bore their only child, Laurel Marie Butterman. She had come too early, her veins spider-webbing beneath the surface of her pale baby skin in a way that left Shiela uneasy about being alone with the baby. After several weeks, she found herself bored with the baby, but enlivened by a fresh curiosity about the domestic life of those mothers at the bus stop. To Sheila Butterman, there was both intrigue and menace about this cadre of women, so polished in their daily routines—hoisting a younger sibling onto a hip, pushing strollers, bringing out lemonade for their children to sell.

For the first time since her childhood, in the absence of work and its subsequent ambition, Sheila Butterman needed a friend. So when Lorraine Diller brought over a silver rattle and bonnet for the infant, Sheila invited her in, let her hold the baby, and accepted Lorraine's invitation to learn Bridge at the Diller's on Wednesday afternoons.

Sheila figured that if the mothers were coiffed at the bus stop, they surely dressed for Bridge. Sheila Butterman, owning no formal attire that wouldn't hold up in court, put on a charcoal gray suit, tucked her infant into her carrier and walked across the street to join Lorraine Diller's Bridge group on a Wednesday afternoon. With Patrick and Howard off to school, Lorraine could rely on bridge to consume great swaths of afternoon and provide an excuse to offer chardonnay and cheese crackers in place of lunch. Lorraine had been hopeful and perhaps cunning about Sheila's company, knowing she'd be disadvantaged for months on account of the learning curve.

Among the other women, Sheila Butterman, *the attorney*, was an anomaly—a career woman who meant business, her hair unstylish but neat, her face unpainted, refusing the wine the other women indulged in. Sheila brought the baby, heated her glass bottles in a pan on the stove, learned quickly and counted cards, standing on no ceremony when she took their quarters hand after hand. She made no friends in these women, save an increased affinity for Lorraine who'd invited her in, allowed her a place at the table and tolerated her relentless victory. Sheila was merely passing time, staving off the boredom that accompanied infant care, though she looked forward to Wednesday afternoons (even weeks after others had soured on her company).

After three months, she announced her gratitude to the assembly of ladies, no longer intriguing nor menacing, and was delighted to return to her career because the baby was finally old enough to be left in capable hands. This was the extent of Sheila Butterman's contact with the Dillers and their sons (whom she'd met only once) until Laurel was grown enough to have strong opinions and interests.

Laurel Butterman grew into a precocious young girl, lightning beneath the skin where veins used to be. She asked risky questions of her nanny who never betrayed her with deceit nor shared her curiosities with the Buttermans even when, perhaps, she should have. Lorne and Sheila did not participate deeply in the rearing of Laurel and were, therefore, content with their enterprise—a daughter who, they believed, had her mother's sense of determination and her father's allegiance to the rules.

By this time, Lorraine Diller had filed for divorce, no longer willing to endure Frank's extramarital interests, and she was looking for opportunities for her young teenaged boys to demonstrate their worth in the world, considering Lorraine was doubting the nature of Frank's. Laurel was just beginning sixth grade and Howard Diller, an awkward boy with pale skin and thin bones, was of perfect age to make sure that Laurel arrived home safely from school and had company until her parents returned from work. Howard wore two keys around his neck—one to his own house and one to the Buttermans who paid him handsomely to turn on the TV and eat Ritz crackers by the sleeve. It was likely that the Buttermans took pity on Lorraine and the boys and furthermore suspected that Howard was an atypical child, the subject of ridicule at school, which explains why very little was expected of him in the hours before they returned home to find no homework completed, Laurel elaborately coiffed and painted like a French doll. He was talented, Sheila would give him that—Laurel's eyes expertly transformed into those of a mannequin: eyelashes curled, lids shadowed in gray, lips red and glossy. And, of course, there was no harm in a little imaginative play.

What the Buttermans didn't know was that Howard also slipped into Sheila's nylons and suit jackets, her pencil skirts and blouses. Howard questioned Laurel about her mother's dim wardrobe. Why didn't she own anything but dull colored suits and chunky heeled pumps? Why and how could she be a self-respecting woman without a few luscious articles to remind her of her success? They had laughed about that—how little her mother needed, how boring it was to play in a closet that offered no fantasy. Howard and Laurel developed a certain space for role play, Howard acting as Laurel's mother, leveling a court decision in which Laurel was found guilty, a sentence issued for kissing a boy, for keeping a dirty room, for failing a test. And sometimes, without

Laurel knowing, Howard slipped into the Butterman's bed. For Laurel, Howard became a proxy for affection while her parents only offered her a warped kind of love—distant and perfunctory. As an adult, Laurel would call this "proximal emotional neglect," never entirely acknowledging what it had done to the woman who had been developing inside her.

It wasn't until Howard was in his late twenties that he started building a collection of shoes and scarves and dresses (from the Macy's sales and the Sears Roebuck clearance area). Self-respecting ladies own an array of shoes and accessories. And, if his mother had been more robust, he would've tried to fit into her blouses and her evening dresses on Sunday evenings, after they'd both had too much brandy to drink and his mother thought it all a curious but acceptable interest and used it as an opportunity to inquire about his personal life. Since, at this time, Howard was openly whatever-he-was, he took advantage of his mother's bounty of jewels and scarves and hats still in boxes, some from a milliner who made custom things for her out on the main-line. His favorite was a pheasant pill box hat that was laid so precisely that it appeared a cock was roosting on his head.

And now, Laurel is home from college visiting her mother who has opinions that still surprise her, and she is watching out the window as Howard and a friend are parading on the sidewalk. Here he is, so thin that the armature of his body beneath the red dress shows his angles—the triangular shape of his torso twisting abstractly in a way Laurel imagines he's learned from watching runway shows. His shoes are noticeably large but still elegant, a peep toe patent pump with a thin ankle strap. His wig is passable, blond. His nails have been manicured. His friend, who has chosen no wig but elaborate make-up, is trailing behind in a purple miniskirt and flouncy top. Howard's legs look incredible: lean and muscular and somehow offensive to Laurel, too.

It's the confident swagger, his lips parted and his jawline rudely angular when she remembers that she had let Howard touch her—kind of. It had happened only once. She had been reading for school—a book about a boy who takes a deer as a pet and whose mother orders him to shoot it, and she'd needed some affirmation that the world was not quite as cruel as the story suggested, when she found Howard in her parents' bed, startled at having been discovered. She had crawled up beside him, her eyes flooding with tears and lay her head on his shoulder. He turned to her and held her and when she'd calmed, he climbed on top of her, placed his knees in the mattress on either side of Laurel's hips. She had not known the words to stop it. In a different home, in a different town, at a different time, with parents who believed in educating their children about the necessity of boundaries, Laurel might've said: *No*, or, *I'll have to tell someone about this*. But instead she said: *You will be a really beautiful woman*, and she let Howard Diller, brown hair in shags at his brow, mauve matte lips (her mother's only color), a slender hand unbuttoning the white silk blouse at his sternum, make the face of a lover in a distant fantasy. She felt him hard against her pelvis as she lay still, afraid and curious. All at once, he was danger and confusion: primal, forsaken. He fingered the smooth flesh of his chest, cast his head to the side. She remembered only his expression in profile, those teeth pronounced and sparkling, an abandonment that frightened her for the will it possessed. He shuddered and gasped, put his fingers to his lips to muffle the surprise sound of exhaustion and shame—a sound that, once Laurel knew sex, would change the way she thought of it, would make her forever silent in ecstasy. He rolled off of her, breathing hard, his lipstick smudged with agitation.

Howard did not come to pick up Laurel from school for the rest of the week. She walked herself home, scanning the sidewalks for Howard, looking for his slight figure in the pizza and coffee shops she passed along the way. Howard knocked on the door that Saturday morning, never stepping inside, telling Sheila Butterman (even as she called for Laurel—*Laurel, honey, Howard's here*) that he'd gotten an apprenticeship with a theater company in the city and would no longer be available after school. Sheila congratulated Howard (*Oh, that's great news, Howard, you're clearly so talented!*) and bid him good luck with his new endeavor. The Buttermans went on to think only occasionally of the Dillers, when they bumped into Lorraine at the grocery store or into Patrick when he came to visit his mother. But it was Howard who seemed to disappear entirely. And it was Laurel who'd not remembered, until now, how Howard Diller had ushered in so many twelve year old curiosities and made them plain, sometimes made them beautiful.

The neighbors have come to gawk at their windows, children and adults and cats and dogs alike, all come to see the spectacle. Shiela puts a hand on Laurel's shoulder as she looks out the window, too.

"Sunday Evening Drag Parade," her mother says.

"Look at his legs. Those muscles," Laurel replies.

"That's an extra short skirt." Her mother raises an eyebrow.

"How long have they been doing this?" Laurel asks. She is home from college where the habits she is developing are reactive, where she allows questions to crack open the sensibilities of a small suburban town.

"Oh, a few years."

"You always knew." Laurel says it as both a statement and a question.

"No. I don't think I did. You did, though, right?" Sheila smooths the bedspread, revising her memory. "He was always different."

"Different than what?"

"The rest of us." Her mother is smirking. Her treatment isn't ridicule exactly, though even at twenty, Laurel is challenged to parse out the difference.

"Come away from the window. You shouldn't gawk." But Laurel senses that Howard and his friend are hoping for an audience. Her mother leaves the room and calls behind her, "Come down for dinner."

"I'm coming," Laurel says, still staring out the window. She inspects Howard's chest, the way he moves confidently even without breasts, the red silk pinned primly at his sternum. He is moving the flowing hem of his dress from side to side with two hands like a can-can dancer, the fabric jumping up above his knees. She puts her hand on the glass and Howard turns, flashing her that sparkling smile she remembers. He tips back his head, brings his shoulder coyly beneath his jawline and waves just the tips of his fingers like a worthy performer. His eyes, unapologetic, say something she cannot hear. Laurel's breath condenses on the window glass, and in it she traces a heart.

Sickness and Health

Ramona hoped to inhabit this house until the young tree in the front yard had grown thick and reached beyond the top of the porch when she would sit at this very angle to consider it. By then, she might be cured of her sickness, if that's what this was—her perfectly acceptable living, her fine family, her children happy enough. Or, this was the onset of middle age: waiting for the slow hand of time to make something big, or if not big, at least admirable of her life, and if not, at least to produce wisdom enough to sit back and regard it.

At her annual check-up, Ramona's doctor had recommended more physical activity. She did walk the dog, of course, and walked the kids to school on days she didn't work. She even walked to neighbors' houses with her bottle of wine and hot appetizer and her smile belying her. But the doctor had recommended she walk with greater intention: more steps, more increased heart rate. She had grown doughy around the middle, and had a history of heart disease, and maybe because this was something that was in her control, she started walking almost every day, with greater intention, usually in the evening, once Rand was home and the kids were tucked in. She found comfort in being by herself, because her husband was unhappy in this house, and leaving him in it, even after the renovation, (which was the kind of project that makes a couple struggle a little, evaluate future economic decisions, the Kantian cost/ benefit with two kids still to put through college) seemed like a triumph of will. She had been frustrated because the project walked along with both of them for the better part of a year, persisting—*What is it that you want?*—and when that project hadn't delivered an answer, she had started taking longer and longer walks, growing a bit more adventurous each time.

At first, she always brought the dog: two miles up Cavanaugh, down Reems, all the way to the end of Joslin where the street dumped into state conservation land and the houses took on a more woodsy, cabin-like feel with big windows and wood burning stoves, then home again. When the dog got spooked by something on Cavanaugh and stopped wanting to go farther than around the block in her known, comfortable neighborhood, she started leaving the dog at home and walking on her own.

Her neighborhood was easy, safe, the kind with block parties and networks of organized people who rallied with their casseroles and their carpools when a new baby arrived, the chemo started, the big storm hit. It was safe enough that good folks routinely left their front and back doors open even during the holidays (perhaps especially during the holidays as if to further endorse the safety they felt there). Ramona herself engaged in the practice.

At the edge of the conservation land, there was a house she admired for its floor to ceiling glass that offered plenty of permission to watch it. It was a house in which she imagined she could live—its warm interior colors persisting through the glass, relentless sunlight and darkness that must've been calculated in its construction.

For days she'd been walking to this house, hoping for a glimpse of its people. She'd posted herself at the edge of the conservation land, watching for the inhabitants to come into the window frame, to show themselves to her, their normal lives, their sickness and health, but they never appeared. Watching the windows was like watching stop animation. Frame one: couch with blanket. Frame two: couch with cat. Frame three: coffee table with empty wine glass.

And tonight, she wasn't even sure why she'd tried the doorknob. It was a risk, to be sure. While Ramona was not prone to risks, she did enjoy the thrill that came in their wake, once the risk had been survived like the roller-coaster let-down, or the long kiss on the elevator before it lurched to a stop and the doors opened on a group of impatient workers returning from lunch. She and Rand used to do that when they first met, before kids, when they lived in the city and could walk to one another's offices and meet for lunch.

She slipped off her Sauconys and left them outside the door—some indicator to outsiders that someone was in the house. She had checked the driveway—no cars this evening as were typical, though she couldn't recall what kind. Predictably, the knob turned easily in her hand, giving way to a black and white floored kitchen, a clean counter, a half-consumed bottle of wine corked and put aside. On the desk was a stack of mail bearing the last name *Sedias: Marjory* and *Bill*. She worked the name through her mouth. *Sa-dee-us* or *Sed-aye-us?* She couldn't be sure, but her heart beat faster, and she clasped her hands together to prevent herself from touching anything. She wondered if trespassing became any less offensive if a person didn't actually touch anything. The cat had found its way into the kitchen and rubbed its feral body against her leg, depositing long peach-colored strands of its hair on her yoga pants. Later, Rand would have a sneezing attack from just those few strands, and she'd let him blame it on the changing of the seasons.

Ramona peeked her head around the door frame to the living room with its spectacular windows, its reading lamp on a timer, casting a small, bright ring on the rust colored sofa. Determining it was empty, she moved into the space, finding a book about adolescent psychology on the coffee table. Now she broke her own rules. She picked it up, leafed through the pages, finding small flags and dog ears and notes in the margins. *Just like J. Ask more detailed questions, not yes/no.* Now she scanned the room for the presence of a teenager. A few photos tucked back on the television console confirmed a couple with children, two boys and a girl, none of them yet teenagers in the photo. The woman was waify with small teeth and hair shaped like a walnut. The man was handsome, bearded with wire framed glasses and a gentle face. Marjory and Bill Sedias.

Ramona was constructing the story: boys away at college, the couple out for the evening, the daughter, perhaps the "J," the challenging adolescent who was the subject of this reading. Whereas before the cat seemed to be following her, now it began to lead, meowing more boldly, showing its sharp teeth and pink tongue, leading her up the narrow, carpeted stairs.

She shouldn't have followed. She knew that. Being caught on the second floor would certainly present a greater challenge of escape, of explanation. But the cat. It was leading her. At the top of the landing, she watched its tail swish around the first doorway. If when Ramona trailed behind it, she would find some semblance of normalcy, the typical clutter of a teenaged daughter's life (notebooks and small trophies, glittered picture frames of friends in braces) *or*, if this were the couples bedroom (a made bed, enough throw pillows to indicate both aesthetic and care, an organized dresser, the closed closet door)—she would be able to leave. She knew that. She had been here long enough. And perhaps then she might have gotten whatever she'd come for. Diagnosis: normal.

She followed the cat around the corner: two twin beds, well made, stood apart. But, this was not a child's room. Two dressers: one male, one female. His and hers. Bill and Marjorie. The kitschy pillows on the bed spelled this out clearly and the sign above the dressers indicated the same: separate beds for separate minds. Maybe one was a restless sleeper or maybe this was a marriage of willful togetherness, like her own parents—a marriage to spare the children the debacle of divorce. Or maybe it was parallel play. Was that what the doctor had called it when her children were very young?

Both closets were open—one revealing a neat row of practical women's shoes and lots of mature looking dresses. This woman must work. This woman must know how to occupy a space. This woman's jewelry rack hung on the back of her closet door, a few long, gold strands glinting in the light. If Ramona were a thief, she would likely take these. The small panic that aligned her thinking with a thief's had her creeping back down the stairs. On the way out, she stopped to uncork the bottle of wine—a quick swig, then another. She paused at the window where a nighttime squirrel was poaching the bird feeder. Someone surely watched this. Marjory or Bill was likely infuriated by the constant refilling of the feeder. But they do not take it down.

That night Rand wanted to touch her and she pretended to be sleeping. Soon she was dreaming of woodland creatures, squirrels running up the thickening tree out front and crawling in through the windows, running along the open beams of her house.

She went out again the next night, and the night after that, with no destination in mind—no house preselected, inviting her in through its windows. She always chose the houses in good condition: tidily kept, in good repair. She estimated that sixty percent of her walks yielded the thrill of entry. She had taken to sitting on the home's couch, reviewing the inhabitants' family photos, leafing through mail, opening kitchen cabinets. Occasionally, she had to urinate. But she was never careless. If she found the toilet seat up, she always returned the seat to its original position. And when she came home, she found her place on her own couch next to Rand, watching college basketball or home renovation programs while she stared blankly and considered the lives of the people who lived in the home she'd visited that evening. She was likely passing the occupants in the aisles of Stop and Shop or speeding past them on Route 1. Rand was likely seeing their ailing dogs and cats at the clinic in town.

At night, Ramona continued to dream of squirrels. That night the squirrels traveled down the interior beams of the house jumping from bedpost to bedpost. They built nests at the foot of her bed, where the dog normally slept. They used their sharp claws to tear through the comforter and hollow out the foam stuffing in the mattress to make room for their bodies to rest alongside one another: a mess of fur and tails. When she made the bed in the morning, she groped for them there, making sure they had not truly nested. She smirked to herself and smoothed the quilt.

That evening, Ramona walked along the west edge of the pond, where the swans sometimes rested, where evidence of carelessness (discarded water bottles, cigarette butts) had been pulled by the ebb of its waters into their nests. Here there were a number of large houses, exposed, in neat square lots with few trees and long driveways. Because of their exposure, these homes were risky. But not if a person looked confident, walked with intent. Because it was dusk and the new moon forgiving, she could walk around the back of a house as if she were an expected guest coming to the back door. This time, she chose to announce herself. It was still light, after all, and people were beginning to return from work. If this home belonged to quiet people who turned off the lights and adjourned to a small portion of the house to read or work, she could explain away her presence. She was sorry, she must have the wrong house, she was looking for the Smiths. The doorbell startled her with its electric zap, like that of a trick hand-buzzer. As was customary, she counted to twenty to prove the home's vacancy before trying the knob.

The back door led, as they often did, to the kitchen, this one in need of remodeling and repairs. The facing on the cabinets had fallen off, exposing a fairly significant stock of canned soup. Ramona detected the vaguest smell of cigarettes.

That's when she heard the low din of a television—a kind of indistinct mumbling like hearing voices through cheap hotel walls. Glancing at the door frame, she could see the faint flicker of bluish light against the semi-gloss paint. Then, a cough: phlegmy and deep. Ramona froze.

"Danny?" called the voice of an older person—raspy and perhaps out of use enough that gender was indistinct to Ramona. She began to panic. She'd never encountered someone at home. She'd perfected her approach: back door, wait time, sneakers off, quiet feet. This time, she'd even rung the bell. Her heart crept up her chest and squeezed in her throat. She could leave at this moment and go undiscovered. But instead, as if propelled by both curiosity and fear, Ramona stepped into the door frame.

"Hello?" the old woman said, clearing her throat. There, in front of Ramona, was a woman of roughly seventy, parked in a wheelchair a few feet from the television, her knobby-knuckled hands folded in her lap. A large, pink-stoned cocktail ring glinted on her finger where a wedding band might be.

"Hello," Ramona answered finally. And then, "Hello," she said again as she took in the woman's thin, gray coiffeur shot through with Technicolor light.

"Is that all you have to say?" the woman asked.

"I... I..." and because she felt challenged, not caught, but challenged and emboldened by her choice to reveal herself, she admitted, "I'm Ramona."

"Well I can see that you're not Danny. Hi, Ramona. I'm Beatrice."

Then the ladies remained locked on one another for some time. The woman examined her, perhaps calculating her next question while Ramona scrambled for an excuse.

"Why don't you come and have a seat. I'm just waiting to see who gets eliminated on this show here, *The Voice*. You watch?"

"Um, no, I don't."

"Come and have a seat then, hon," the woman said again, motioning in a vague way to the room behind her.

Ramona entered cautiously, noticing how the heavy velvet curtains prematurely darkened the room. The small sofa was lined with brocade pillows, so Ramona sat down in the rocking chair over the woman's left shoulder.

The woman continued, "The show's simple enough. They sing, they get coached and get cut. You know the drill. I can't get enough of that Adam Levine. So handsome."

Ramona surveyed the room—a collection of small silver spoons was mounted to the wall in a case made especially for that purpose. The coffee table offered a candy dish filled with starlight mints. They did not speak while the show concluded, the young woman in a sequined pant suit was eliminated from the pack.

"Goodbye to Jocelyn. Never liked her anyway. Neither did Adam." The woman flicked off the television and maneuvered the wheelchair to face Ramona.

"How about a snack? I was waiting for Danny, but, if you don't mind… There's cheese in the fridge, crackers to the left of the sink. A glass of water would be great."

And because this woman didn't question her, didn't *need* to question her (a condition that Ramona found both safe and unmooring) she retreated to the kitchen and began finding her way.

Ramona called back to the living room, "And who is Danny?"

"My brother."

"Oh. And you're expecting him?"

"Eventually."

"Today?"

"He comes once a day. Why? You nervous?"

"Just curious. Why did you invite me in?"

"I didn't invite you, if you remember. But you're here. And I like company."

Ramona finished arranging the cheese and crackers on a cutting board she found behind the toaster. She filled two glasses with water, found a couple of decorative cocktail napkins in a drawer and brought out the tray to the living room.

When Ramona reappeared, the woman seemed surprised. "You spoil me," the woman said as Ramona set down the tray. If she wanted to leave, could she do it now? Tell her, *Here's your snack. Nice to meet you.* It was probable that she could leave without getting further involved. The woman might even reply, *Goodbye Ramona. Nice to meet you.*

That's when she noticed the woman's feet poking out from beneath the multi-colored afghan. They were bare; swollen reddish-purple toes overlapped one another, the nails yellowed and overgrown. The woman proceeded to alternate a bite of cheese then a bite of cracker, a sip of water.

"Good cheddar that Dubliner. Aged just the right amount of time."

Ramona nodded, glancing again at the woman's feet.

"Well, are you going to join me?" the woman asked.

Ramona chose a piece of cheese and sat down again at the edge of the rocking chair, being certain not to settle in too deeply.

The woman held the crackers in the palm of her hand so that Ramona noticed what looked like discolored callouses on her fingertips. The black case that lay on the coffee table was open, revealing a small meter and a vial of liquid. Cracker, cheese, water, cracker, cheese, water. The woman dabbed at her lips quite daintily from time to time.

They munched in silence.

"You're awfully quiet for a person who comes unannounced."

Ramona could feel her face flushing red. She managed a sheepish smile.

Now the woman sat back in her wheelchair. "I needed that. Feeling much better now. My blood sugar was low."

"Are you a diabetic?"

"Forty years." She lifted the afghan from her feet to reveal the symptoms. "Caught you looking at them. If I'd known you were coming, I'd have put on my slippers."

"Don't bother. I'm sorry. I should be going."

"Oh don't let me scare you away. You smoke?"

"No. Never have."

"Turns out I like you anyway. Now, if you wouldn't mind wheeling me out on the deck, I'll have a smoke before you go."

Again, the woman gestured in a vague way toward a screen door that led outside. Because this woman spoke as if she couldn't be denied, Ramona grabbed hold of the wheelchair and, having never pushed a wheelchair before, found navigating it through the doorframe and onto the deck easier than she'd anticipated. Outside, the deck was shrouded by trees, protecting them from the dimming sun. The neighbor's magnolia had dropped fleshy petals on the porch that bruised under the weight of her footsteps and the wheelchair's thin wheels.

"Near the far corner post please," the woman said as Ramona wheeled her toward the railing. Ramona positioned the woman so that they both could look out into the neighbor's garden which had just begun to flower with phlox and snowmound spirea. The woman reached up and removed the wooden corner cap from the railing to reveal a pack of Parliaments and a book of matches hidden there.

She lit one and drew in a deep breath.

"I like to watch the squirrels. They wrestle in that tree there." She exhaled. "Almost like acrobats."

Then Ramona heard the skittering and scratching, a feral noise like glee and ferocity and spite. Like stuntmen, two squirrels tumbled down the trunk, catching hold of one another even as they flipped and writhed and looked as if they might fall. The woman continued to pull on her cigarette. It was curious to Ramona that even after all this, after *The Voice* and cheese and crackers and a cigarette, that she hadn't asked a thing about Ramona—for what reason she'd come, where she lived, or even why she'd taken off her shoes.

It was evening now, the sun creeping toward the horizon. She should surely be going. She wanted to think that Rand would start to worry. But he never did. That's when she heard a door opening, the sound of footsteps, a thumb pressing the screen door handle. This must be Danny.

"Bea, who's here?" he asked, finding the two of them out on the porch. The man scanned her from head to toe, finding her shoeless and looking surprised.

"This is Rachel. She's a friend of mine. Rachel, this is Danny."

"Pleasure," Ramona said, waving subtly. Danny nodded. Ramona shot the woman a look that she deflected without emotion.

"You're smoking again. Bea, how many times…"

The woman shot back, "Aww Danny cut it out. We were just watching the squirrels. And you're late."

"I'm not late. I was here earlier. Came back to check your sugar."

She looked distant. "It was fine. I checked myself."

"What was the number?"

The woman raised her eyebrows to signal fatigue.

"What was the number? You don't remember, do you?" He asked again.

The woman glanced at Ramona. "Danny, you're being rude."

"Tell me the number," he demanded.

"Two twenty."

The man turned toward Ramona now and asked, "Did she check it?"

Ramona found herself nodding.

"I should be going," Ramona said as she turned toward the woman and took her gnarled hand in hers. "I'll see you soon, Bea. Ok?"

The woman drew Ramona's hand close and whispered into their entire history which seemed to expand consequentially to a place of stewardship and protection—"Don't leave me now. I like your company."

Ramona felt the sharpness of the woman's cocktail ring in her palm. "I'll let you have your visit. Don't worry. I'll come again soon." Ramona meant it. She knew that.

Ramona thanked her for her snacks, her company, offered pleasantries to Danny who was whittling down the consciousness of his sister. And even as the screen door slapped close, maybe the woman was guessing and second-guessing Ramona's arrival and presence, or perhaps she was thinking of her not at all, perhaps she'd already forgotten, eliminated her, like the woman in the sequined pant suit. Perhaps the woman was only hoping that Rachel (Ramona), or some kind or neutral and otherwise harmless woman might come to watch the squirrels with her, might make her a cheese plate and keep her company and offer some version of herself regardless of the conditions. She wondered, if when she went to visit in the coming days, if Beatrice would call her by her real name.

Ramona walked home the way she'd come, past the swans and the public pool. Ramona's feet were quiet and did not disturb the community of rabbits that were sitting still in front lawns and twitching about in garden beds—vigilantes for the quiet and the conscious. They did not flinch as she passed, their stillness was both expectant and fearful, waiting to see what this woman might do. Would she approach them, or move swiftly past? Their feet were triggers to retreat in a flash, white tails like jet trails streaking across the lawn.

At the skate park, the skateboarders were getting in their final attempts at the half pipe, sliding in limber piles of bones and skin at the base of the pipe, their shaggy hair falling across their faces. At the tennis courts, a doubles team of seniors were shaking hands and wiping the sweat from their brows.

Cavanaugh was quiet. She passed no dog walkers or runners, no stroller-pushing parents out to soothe a cranky evening baby. Ramona approached home and noticed that the young trunk of the tree had fattened considerably in the spring rain, the leaves still not yet reaching above the porch. She climbed the stairs and was startled to find Rand there, sitting in the porch swing waiting for her, a heavy glass in his hand.

"You've been gone a long time. I was worried."

Ramona slid in next to him and put her head on his shoulder. "Long walk," she said.

He handed her his drink. She sipped. He drew his arm around her. Across the street, the Maguire's dog went suddenly wild at the illusive shadows in the yard.

"The tree is getting bigger, finally," Rand said. By fall when they'd sit here, the leaves of the tree would curl into long cigarettes before dropping to the ground at winter's onset. By then, the squirrels would have completed their hard work, making a treasure trove of acorns in the front yard. By then, they would've found their way, set up an encampment outside Ramona's bedroom window, dragging remnants of food and other foraged items up the trunk of the fattening tree and onto their roof. Ramona would watch the squirrels tussle, making known their territory to one another, scaring the others off who were encroaching on their space. Ramona would open her window, lift out the screen as an invitation.

Their rhythmic, twitching tails, their nests lined with what is left behind: dryer lint, a burnt bagel and a bottle cap, the ferns from a prom corsage. The discarded, the neglected, the lost, the squirrels scrapping hard to bring it home, to make use of it regardless of its origin.

Pie

If it weren't for the western facing porch and Francine Morrow's pastry skills, and the jet stream, too, I suppose, I wouldn't know a thing about pie. My daughter made a project of refurbishing the wicker porch furniture, so recently I've taken to reading the paper out there with the superb exposure and the rash of temperate late-summer days. And Francy continues to bake pies when the breeze is slow and accommodating enough to carry their buttery loveliness in gentle waves through the screen and into my olfactories. What is a man to do? I have lost my patience.

I can't keep General from digging in Francy's flower beds, a habit he started after Evelyn passed, digging for a bone he never buried. He drags himself home after being scolded, dirt in his nostrils, slobbering mud. And if it weren't for him, I might be able to earn a piece out of commiseration or brief companionship. Francy and I—just a couple of pie-eating widows, we could joke.

The thing with pie is, you can't just bake a piece. You bake a whole one, keep a substantial yet respectable wedge for yourself, and then what? Deliver it, make peoples' days with it, fill in their loneliness. I've watched her march across the street to the Lonergan's place with its perfectly angular hedges trimmed every Monday by Therese, the anorexic-looking wife. I've watched the wife's forearms, thin like dowels, take in the pie, knowing it's a burden to her, that it will be wasted. Pie must be relished. I would eat it for breakfast or, gladly, for dinner with a glass of wine. Even Evelyn would have approved of pie for dinner. But instead, I've been condemned only to smell it.

Evelyn's wake had been a catered affair, save for Francy Morrow's cherry pie which she brought in sympathy and which I thought was a bold choice. The dish was still warm when she placed it in my hands. I considered hiding it in the pantry for private consumption, but my daughter, Meredith, put it out with the pound cake and the tea sandwiches and I never got a bite. Francy had been one of the last to leave and before she walked back across the street, she hugged me, not just with sympathy, but with the kind of affection one reserves for circumstances when misfortune precipitates new affinity. The smell of butter was still in her hair.

Sunday marked the first anniversary of Evelyn's passing. Meredith had me for dinner as she has done every Sunday this past year, a routine about which we both feel fairly ambivalent, I'm sure. Like Evelyn, Meredith doesn't cook. So as I bit into a cooling egg roll, grease dribbling down my stubbled chin, Meredith made the proclamation—"You're recuperated," she said. Like all it took was a year of take-out and some feigned quality-time to bring me back. "You should enjoy yourself," she said which made me fail to protest that I was. She sent me home with new couch pillows, yellow and white feminine things that were not particularly comfortable but that I placed on the freshly painted wicker nonetheless. Her brother sent me an iPad and a note that read: *Hear ur well- wlkg! These gadgets r gr8. Luv, J (and Maura).* Maura was the new girl who wore dresses in my company as if out of respect for another time. Even if she wore dresses for Jason, or even for herself, liberated woman that she seemed, I liked her.

I *had* been walking. My cholesterol was down to 175. I sometimes took General to Spot Pond where I threw the tennis ball into the water and watched his black body bobbing like an empty oil drum on the surface. Just a few days prior to my children-certified recuperation, I left General behind and asked Francy to join me on a walk to the center of town. At my invitation, she smiled in the sideways manner of a person who cannot conceal their presumptions.

I was grateful that she kept a good pace. She chatted away about her present life, checking me in the corner of her eye like a nervous schoolgirl. We did not talk about my wife or her late husband, Henry. But somewhere along the way, smitten by my company, the delight of this surprise, she'd turned the fullness of her face to mine so that I was sure she had grown enamored of me and said, "Well, Frank, isn't this a delight?" Perhaps, then, it was my silence that spoiled the outing. She was attractive, I'd always thought so, and I suppose we made a handsome couple, a memorable one that younger observers might consider quite a bit younger in age than we actually were.

Though I remained silent, I was considering her beyond the prospect of pie when we walked through the farmer's market in full swing. She didn't even glance at the quarts of berries calling to be nestled between perfectly tender folds of flaky dough. Her eyes were trained on my face so that I wondered if she was trying to find her late husband there. And, I suppose, I let her down doubly because I looked nothing like Henry and because when I forced two quarts of the Maine blues into her hands saying, "These will make the most delectable pie," she wrinkled her eyebrow and let out the kind of low moan a person does when they've lost something dear.

We started home then, a wide swath of silence between us, her face tipped toward the ground, while I thought of ways to ignite the baker spirit in her. I said, "It's great to be really good at something. You know, like I am at games. I love to watch Jeopardy. You must have something you love doing like that."

She denied having any kind of talent at all. If I'd mentioned the baking, it would've been too leading, too much of a summons to maintain any subtlety or grace. I suggested her gardening was quite exquisite, but she mentioned General, how he'd been digging in her flower beds. At the door, I became desperate and, forcing the heaping quarts into her hands said, "I'd like to get these berries into one of your pies," or some such thing. She turned the doorknob and went inside.

She slid a note in my mailbox the following day that said: *Mr. Cronholm, Hank always said, "Gentlemen can't be made. When I'm gone, don't waste your time with anyone who isn't." I shall heed his advice. Regards, Mrs. Henry Morrow.* That was our last exchange.

Since then, I have endured exactly twelve days of incessant baking. It's August. Kitchens are sweltering. Most ovens are off. She intends for this to be my pie purgatory. And now, just as chemistry is doing its part, just as the smell of fresh butter is turning to a nuttier, browner smell but just before I can detect with which fruit it is filled, I have a new plan.

If it's bush berry, my plan will make the most sense. If it's peach or rhubarb (though rhubarb would've gone to wood by now), my plan will be less plausible. If it's candy pie (an abomination in my mind), I'll lose faith in her forever.

I fold the newspaper into fourths and then neatly into eighths. I rise from the glider, shoulders first, forcing my back to hunch and my neck to hang just slightly, thinking about the two bears at the local zoo. I let my arms freely dangle as I lumber out of the room. I stand before the hall mirror where I realize I look more like a gorilla than a bear. It's the arms, I think. Bears aren't bipedal by nature. They rear up only when fighting. What might a bear be doing with his arms? Eating honey, I think. Picking berries, I think. Shaking trees. But, I don't want to frighten her.

I consult the encyclopedias that collect dust in the den. I take one of my plump fingers and drag it down the reference page until I find *bear: large mammal of the family Ursidae in the order Carnivora, found almost exclusively in the Northern Hemisphere.* Indeed, I think. *They stand on hind feet to reach objects with their paws. Nearly all species are omnivorous, feeding on fruits* (like the kind that come in pie), *roots and other plant matter...* Two pictures accompany the entry. One shows a bear standing on hind legs, its shiny patent nose wet with anticipation. The other shows a bear mid-lope, in pursuit on all fours, the slackened skin of its belly swinging between its legs. I smooth my hands over my own belly, the buttons of my shirt straining to contain it. General watches, mystified, his head cocked at two o'clock as I amble out the door and across the street to Francy's place. Now, the smell is clear. Triple berry pie: a blend of tart blackberries, raspberries and sweet blues. A bear's dream. I knock on her door.

Through the window, I watch her wipe her hands on her juice-stained apron as she approaches. She hesitates a moment and then speaks through the glass, "What is it, Frank?"

"Well, good afternoon, Francine," I say. "It would be ever so un-gentlemanly of me to trouble you, and yet I must."

"Are you here to apologize?"

"I suppose I am, yes." I hang my head and slacken my face, giving it a quick shake from side to side as I imagine bears often do when they are shooing a fly from their face. I set my arms at a clumsy obtuse angle. I accentuate the protrusion of my gut, and say, "It's just that I'm part bear, you see."

"Pardon?" she says.

"If you wouldn't terribly mind opening the door, I'll explain everything."

"I most certainly will not, Mr. Cronholm! Did my note not make my position perfectly clear?"

"Oh, yes. Well, of course. But Francine, it's just that I haven't been perfectly honest with you." At my overture, she unlatches the chain lock and opens the door a fraction. Her face softens just slightly. Her cheeks are flushed from the warmth of the kitchen and I almost reconsider.

"Bears have needs, too," I say.

"Oh, Frank. Please!" She shuts the door again.

"Francine, if it weren't for your exquisite pies and my acute sense of smell, I wouldn't be here at all. It's just that, I am a solitary being, as bears are, and I do not feed with others except where large quantities of food are available. Otherwise, I have little social contact."

"Clearly!"

"I spent most of last winter sleeping in the den upstairs and with the approaching winter, I am sure to do the same."

"Frank, you have quite the nerve," she says pointing at me through the glass. "If it's a piece of pie you want, why don't you ask?"

I straighten my spine, allow my body to return to upright posture, my mind to return to the fallible, despicable, pie-eating man I am and, humbled, say, "Well, Mrs. Francine Cronholm, I have the good fortune of smelling your exquisite pies from my reading spot across the street and I'd be ever so honored if you would share a slice with me in the sunshine of this glorious afternoon."

"No!" she shouts, jabbing a greasy finger at the glass. "Pie of this prestige is reserved for gentlemen only, not bears or cheats or fakes. Promptly remove yourself from my porch."

Her face dissolves to hopelessness. It is clear she cannot find a shred of Henry's resemblance in anything about me, so I take myself the long way home, around the side of her house where the kitchen windows face the garden. There, I find the golden grail of pies sitting on the sill. And with my thick limbs, I reach up to the sill, scoop out a heaping, steaming mound of crust and berries with one clumsy paw. I bury my face in it, break off a moon of brown crust, the impressions of Francy's thumbs crushing softly between my teeth. It is just how I imagined it. No, it is better. There are seeds in my teeth, juice rimming my mouth, berry bruises on my shirt. My belly is round and warm and full. I lope home.

Acknowledgments

Gratefully acknowledged are the following publications, where certain stories first appeared in earlier versions:

"The Unseen" (formerly "Those Unseen") in *Front Porch*

"C3PGirl" in *The Los Angeles Review*

"Cicadas" in *The Kenyon Review*

"Up Dell Drive" in *Water~Stone Review*

* * *

I took a leap when I left teaching full-time to finish this book. Deep gratitude to my husband, Matt, and my daughters who were both patient and supportive these many years, telling people I was writing a book even as I pressed my finger to my lips to quiet them. While I am a solitary and private thinker and writer, my husband sometimes asks exactly the right questions at the right time without dashing the art from the work.

This book wouldn't be possible without the outstanding staff at Cornerstone Press—namely Dr. Ross Tangedal and Ellie Atkinson, who were patient, deferential, and, overall, delightful to work with. Also, a huge thanks to Cornerstone's Sophie McPherson in sales and Ava Willett in media and proofreading. Teaching presses are amazing. Thank you, also, to my publicist, Kait Astrella.

I'd like to thank my parents for their enduring encouragement and faith in my ability, which I've often doubted but cherished these many years. To my grandfather, F. David Martin, who read much of my early writing and who would have been so proud to hold this book in his hands.

I'd like to thank my writing and literature teachers over the years: Roberta Simms at Bucknell University where I took creative writing as an ambitious high school student. To the community of wonderful teachers at Kenyon College and later at Vermont College of Fine Arts (Jess Row, Larry Sutin, Robert Vivian, Abby Frucht), all of whom offered their time and encouragement on some of these stories and invariably prompted others that haven't yet been written. Later, I'd learn from teachers like Neema Avashia and Anna Godberson, whose teachings ring in these pages, too.

To the editors at the literary journals, who published many of these stories: A.J. Ortega at *Front Porch Journal*, Kelly Davio at *The Los Angeles Review*, Mary Rockcastle at *Water~Stone Review*, and David Lynn at *The Kenyon Review*. It means a great deal to be recognized for your story-telling, especially early in one's career. Thanks for keeping my chin up.

To Emily (Sauber) Logan, for being my first friend who understood how much the written word meant to both of us.

To Robin MacArthur and Jennifer Bowen Hicks, who I met at VCFA but who have sustained the conversation, the friendship and writership these many, many years. I am forever grateful for our conversations, however infrequent. I'd meet you anywhere.

To the group of Melrose writers (especially Elizabeth, Jane, Jane, Lisa, and Anne, and formerly Acacia, Jen and Lori) with whom I've developed a sense of writerly community and friendship, and who have been gracious enough to lend their ear to my novel in progress.

Finally, a deep debt of gratitude to my students, past and future, who, I realize, are the original inspiration for many of these stories; and to all people dwelling at the limen (however temporarily): you are brave and beautiful and vulnerable, too. I see you.

Sara Reish Desmond's work has appeared in *The Kenyon Review*, *The Los Angeles Review*, and *Water~Stone Review*, among other journals. Her short stories have been finalists for the Rick DeMarinis Short Story Award and the Copper Nickel Award. She teaches and writes just north of Boston, where she lives with her husband and two daughters.

Printed in the USA
CPSIA information can be obtained
at www.ICGtesting.com
CBHW032203221024
16268CB00025B/307